RANCHER ON THE LINE

BARB HAN

TORJAKE PUBLISHING

To my family for unwavering love and support. I can't imagine doing life with anyone else. I love you guys with all my heart.

1

D ane Firebrand didn't shy away from a fight. Not in the fifth grade when a kid three years his senior bullied his best friend; not against his twin cousins when they'd decided to gang up on him once in middle school; and not against countless enemies seen and unseen during his time in Kandahar. So, why now? Why did he feel the need to retreat from his family's ranch before anyone spotted him?

The July heat hit with full force. Sweat beaded on his forehead. And yet it was nothing compared to what he'd experienced at Bagram. *This* was doable. It didn't hurt there were no dangerous dirt roads, bombs, or terrorists to contend with in Lone Star Pass. All he planned to do while in Texas was pay his respects for a grandfather he grew up around but couldn't say he knew or respected. Marshall Firebrand didn't get close to anyone as far as Dane remembered. The man had done his level best to divide the family, which he'd excelled at, and now that he was gone, Dane doubted that anything would change.

This trip would be in and out, a couple of days max. He

owed his mother that much, considering he'd only come home a handful of times over the years and never stayed long enough to wear out his welcome. Dreading it to this degree caught him off guard.

Tonight, he needed a place to stay. The home that had been built for him on ranch property would be too obvious. There would be no flying under the radar until he was ready to make an appearance if he stayed there.

Come on, man. The whole reason he'd come home was to show his face before moving on to a permanent location. Why was he struggling so much?

He issued a sharp sigh, not ready to unpack the answer to his question. The cabin owned by his best friend's family would provide a good cover until he could get his bearings. Jacob wouldn't mind, having enacted an open-door policy a long time ago. Taking a day to get his bearings shouldn't be a problem. His family might know he was on his way home, but he didn't commit to a date. He'd been cooling off on a former tobacco farm in Virginia, waiting for clearance to rejoin society. What would one more day hurt?

The familiar burn in his right hand caused him to flex and release his fingers. Nerve damage was for the birds. IEDs were for the birds. Being home was for the...

Before he went headfirst down that rabbit hole again, he walked over to his rental sedan, opened the door, and claimed the driver's seat. No one would recognize the vehicle, which would buy him even more time. Plus, he had no plans to park in front of Jacob's place. The fishing cabin would be empty now that his friend's family had moved to Houston to be closer to an aunt. He knew the layout like the back of his hand so moving around without a light on wouldn't be a problem. He'd park his rental in a safe spot nearby. All things considered, a decent last-minute plan.

Dane stayed lost in thought on the drive. At close to midnight, there were no other vehicles on the road. He cut off headlights as he neared the fishing cabin, a place he could get to from memory after all the summers he and Jacob had spent there after chores, of course. To get any kind of freedom, Dane's work had had to be done, responsibilities that took up most of the day, six days a week while growing up. Much of the time, Jacob would sneak over to help to buy time for them to hang out.

Dane would never know why so many of his brothers and cousins had stayed on to work the land and play constant mediator to a father who never had time for them and an uncle who was just as bad. Most of his good childhood memories happened off the cattle ranch and away from his family. In places like this.

There were half a dozen cabins on this stretch of road. At one time, he'd personally known the owners of each one. Now, he was only certain about the last three belonging to the Reeds, Jacob's, and the Meirs. As he passed the Reed family cabin, he noticed a vehicle parked to the side. A glow came from the master bedroom window. He didn't, and wouldn't, recognize the two-door convertible sedan. For all he knew, the family could be renting the place out now that the internet made it available with one click. If memory served, there was a small opening in the trees in between Jacob's and the Meir's cabins. Teenagers used to park there for privacy. It had been so long since Dane had been here, the place could be grown over by now.

He rolled on past Jacob's place toward the Meir's. There were no streetlights on the gravel road. He risked flashing his fog lights and saw the opening right where he remembered it to be. The little spot was still there. And that was the first bit of comfort he'd experienced since arriving in town five hours ago and hiding out on his family land.

Ditching the black, four-door sedan would be easy for now, especially under the cover of night. He may have to find a better place for it at first light. Or, better yet, drag some downed tree branches over for cover.

Dane grabbed his rucksack from the backseat and locked up the vehicle, his step a little lighter now that he'd bought himself more time. He pressed a button to start the timer on his watch. It was important to know how long it would take to get back to his escape vehicle. The move was habit at this point, and probably unnecessary in a small town like Lone Star Pass, but it could mean life or death where he'd spent the last seventeen years. Here in the civilian world, there probably wasn't the need to know that if he walked this in four minutes and fifty-two seconds then he could run it in a hair over one minute flat. The knowledge only served to remind him that he'd forgotten what it was like to be anything but a soldier.

Now that he'd medically boarded out, his new plan was to stay away from as many people as possible until he figured out how to be a civilian again.

Dane tried the door of the two-bedroom cabin. Locked? That was a first. Or maybe it had just been that long since he'd been back. Did he expect everything to be the same as before he left? The short answer? Yes. As unrealistic as the thought might be, he'd had it just the same. He was starting to realize the saying about never being able to go home again might be more accurate than he'd given credit.

While slipping his hand inside his rucksack, another thought occurred to him. If people used locks, they might have alarms now too. He gripped the universal key, deciding to investigate. He moved around the building, peering in room after room. The last thing he needed was Sheriff Lawler making an appearance tonight, full-on lights, alerting everyone to Dane's presence. There was nothing like disturbing his neighbor to help him make a new friend.

Room by room, Dane checked for the telltale red dot on a wall or near a door to indicate Jacob's family had put in an alarm system. Dane was beginning to think he should have called, but then that would be another first.

There were no dots to be found. He circled the cabin once more just to be certain there were no more surprises; his eyes had long ago adjusted to the dark. Being outside meant being more in his element than he cared to admit. Being alone in the woods, near one of his favorite fishing holes, brought back a flood of good memories he'd forced out of his mind. Had he blocked out all the good from Lone Star Pass along with the bad?

Leaving this place and getting as far away from his feuding relatives as possible had been the right move. Besides, he couldn't imagine working a cattle ranch the rest of his life. The job had been forced down his throat as a kid where he'd worked long hours with little reprieve. Hard work wasn't the problem. Lack of choice about how and when he worked was.

Dane slipped the universal key inside the lock. He twisted and jiggled it a couple of times before hearing the telltale snick. He shouldered his rucksack, opened the door, and made a move to step inside.

A tree branch snapped to the left, not fifteen feet away. Dane slipped into soldier mode, crouching low to the floor while placing his rucksack next to the door without making so much as a sound. He pulled out and then unsheathed his Ka-Bar knife, the stacked leather handle feeling a little too natural against his palm as he closed his fingers around it.

The seven-inch blade was sharp enough to trim the hair on the back of his hand, so imagine what it could do to a person's skin.

Dane intentionally left the door open and waited. Patience won battles. And he'd been one of the best soldiers.

CATALINA IVEY FROZE.

Less than ten minutes ago she'd heard gravel crunch underneath tires. She'd thrown off her covers and ducked into the second bedroom of her rental where it was dark with one question...had she been caught? She'd made it to the window in time to catch the blacked-out car as it inched past the cabin. Fear had seized her.

Still in yoga pants and a sports bra, she'd thrown on an oversized t-shirt and slipped into her running shoes, which were positioned beside the door just in case. Being constantly on guard was becoming second nature. She'd been careful. She'd taken every precaution she could think of, renting the cabin in cash, making a fake ID and renting the convertible from a small dealership. Nothing should tie her to this place. Had they found her?

Frustration nipped as she'd bolted through the tree line, keeping the vehicle in view. The minute it had diverted off the gravel path, she'd known she was in trouble.

Trekking back slowly toward her rental, curiosity and fear got the best of her. She'd stopped at the cabin in between the vehicle and hers, and waited to get a good look at the driver. The blacked-out vehicle tipped her off to the fact this person was not on a family vacation.

Thick trees formed a screen in between each cabin to afford plenty of privacy. It had been a main selling point for the place and one of the many reasons she'd chosen this location. The Wi-Fi was spotty but she made do. In fact, her former boss would rule out looking for her in an area like this because of it. Being discovered was not an option. And here she'd been so careful in the past week since arriving, keeping a low profile. Even a sharp sigh couldn't rid her of her frustration—frustration at having to lose precious time relocating when all she wanted was to be with her infant son.

Adrenaline thumping, her fight, flight, or freeze response kicked on high alert. This was a complication she couldn't afford. She still had too much code to write. The app would never get up and running at this rate. This nightmare would never end.

Catalina half expected to get caught at some point. She just didn't anticipate being found this fast. Her ready bag was always packed just like Lucas had taught her. In fact, she was pretty much relying on all his war stories for guidance at this point. They were the reason she'd made it through the past three weeks after realizing her boss had other plans with the pet project she was developing. She remembered like it was yesterday. She'd put on a smile, gotten through her workday, and then wiped out her computer's hard drive before walking out.

Since then, she'd secured the one thing that meant most to her in the world and had gone on the road. Frustration nipped at her because she was inching along with writing the code, making some progress at least. She'd already found five bugs and fixed two.

She wasn't sure how long she could outrun Tech Corp. A little voice reminded her she'd be on the road forever if she didn't finish this code and get it in the right hands. She knew exactly who to sell it to...the competition.

Catalina knew for a fact Hanson Tech would do the right thing with the app. But she couldn't do anything until she finished. Once she had the finished product, and therefore a bargaining chip, she could take it to Hanson himself and then there would be no reason for her former boss to come after her. Hanson could provide protection no one else could. All she had to do was keep herself alive long enough to finish.

She froze, standing so still that no one would even hear her breathe as she caught sight of a dark figure.

Panic seized her chest. She'd walked too slowly, been too careful, and the driver of the vehicle had beaten her to the cabin. Curiosity had gotten the best of her when she wanted to know what he looked like, who they'd sent.

Her eyes now adjusted to the dark, she saw a hulk of a man step inside the cabin. She listened for the sound of the door closing, locking. It never came. Catalina gripped the mesquite tree where she'd been standing several minutes now, waiting for a light to come on inside the cabin. Wouldn't there be a light?

She took a slow step to the side, and then back without making so much as a sound. She risked another, fighting the instinct to turn toward her rental and run. She could only hope that coming to Lone Star Pass hadn't been the critical mistake she feared it might turn out to be. Lucas's friend was from here. Tears threatened at the thought of Lucas even though it had been a year. *Gone too soon.*

A few more minutes ticked by. She heard nothing, not one sound other than chirps and clicking noises from insects in the trees. She figured it was safe to turn around and head back to her cabin.

Once there, she needed to grab her laptop, throw it inside her ready bag, and get out of Dodge.

As she turned, she practically slammed into a wall. It was immediately clear she'd just stepped into a man.

"What are you doing, spying on me?" The man's voice was a low, angry rumble. She ignored the vibration of attraction it caused to rocket through her body. Fear could do the same thing to a person, excite the nervous system and cause a response that mirrored attraction. This was no different.

In the heat of the moment, his actual words barely registered. All she could think about was getting far away from this person. She couldn't afford to get caught or have her identity revealed. More than her life was on the line and the temporary arrangement she'd made for her son wouldn't last forever. Tucking Luke away and far from her was the hardest thing she'd ever done. Ripping her heart out of her chest couldn't be for nothing, and she couldn't allow herself to consider never going home again. There was no backup plan for Luke being brought up by someone else. The only living relative she stayed in contact with, her granny, was too old to take in an infant for the long haul. Granny might be independent now, but she wouldn't be forever. The very real possibility she wouldn't be around to see Luke's first day of kindergarten stabbed Catalina in the chest. If she didn't find a way out of this mess, her precious son might end up in foster care, brought up by strangers.

The thought fueled her. She pushed off the Hulk and tried to take off in the opposite direction. His hand clasped around her wrist, creating a steel vise, stopping her dead in her tracks. She balled her fists, lifted her hand as high as she could before dropping it down in one swift motion. Nothing.

When the next move didn't work, she dropped down to her knees. Or, at least, she attempted to. The hulk of a man didn't give her an inch. He brought his other hand up to grip her forearm, holding her in place in front of him.

"You didn't answer my question." His voice was akin to a volcano erupting, threatening to cause the same amount of damage.

There was no way she was giving away the sound of her voice. He wasn't getting any more information than he already had. She had to think.

Think. Think. Think.

Since her arms were of no use, she brought her knee up, angled the heel of her foot at his shins and fired off a kick. Her heel connected, and, pain shot through her foot. Somehow, she figured she was the one who took the most damage. He grunted, clearly not amused, but her heel screamed in pain.

Out of nowhere, he chuckled, causing all kinds of rage to fuel her next move—a move she gave no thought to. Instead, she went as wild as she could, holding back nothing. Who laughed at pain? Keeping the image of her son in her arms close to her thoughts, she gripped Hulk's arms. Trying to turn the tables on him, she dug her fingernails into his flesh. At the same time, she stomped on his foot before drawing her knee up to land where no man wanted to be struck.

He took a step back just in time to avoid contact.

Catalina let out a yell that would rival any wild animal as she twisted and wriggled her body, trying to break free from his grasp.

"I'll give you want you want. I'll let you go." His voice was a study in calm despite the barrage she'd unleashed on him.

Then the first words he'd spoken to her started to sink in. *What are you doing, spying on me?*

Would someone from Tech Corp ask this question? Reason crept in, whereas she'd been running on pure adrenaline and emotion. Was it possible he had nothing to do with her former employer?

"Why were you driving down the road without your lights on?" she asked, breaking her no-talking rule.

"*That*?" He sounded shocked. "I didn't want to be seen and I was trying to be polite." The calmness was gone from his voice, replaced with irritation. "If you would calm down, we could talk like adults."

Polite? The very real fear she'd misread the situation loomed like a rain-heavy cloud. If she wanted to stay at the cabin, and she did, she was going to have to do some fast talking to explain herself.

2

"Sorry, I-uh," the woman's gaze darted around like she was searching for an escape route, "thought you might be an ax murderer or sadistic rapist." This person wasn't much taller than five feet four inches but was surprisingly strong and had a few maneuvers that made him believe she'd at the very least taken a martial arts class. Dane half figured the digs on his arms from her fingernails were bleeding and don't even get him started on the near-miss with her knee to his groin.

"My name is Dane Firebrand. I'd appreciate it if you kept it between us." He figured sharing something about himself might put her at ease. He truly felt bad if she believed what she'd just said. It also told him she was most likely staying at the cabin next door by herself, which would explain her reaction to him.

"Wait," she said, sounding like she'd just seen a ghost. "You're Dane Firebrand? Stetson?"

"How do you know that nickname?" Dane took a step back, trying to get a better look at the woman. His eyes were slowly adjusting to the darkness. The fact she didn't offer her name didn't get past him.

"I knew one of your close friends." Her voice caught on the last word and it seemed to take her a few seconds to be able to keep her emotions in check. "You're the reason I'm here."

"What does that mean?" Now he really was confused. No one knew he was coming except for family and they didn't even know when he planned to arrive. "Are you looking for me or something? Because I can promise you we've never met."

Dane could count on one hand the number of folks who called him Stetson, and none of them were from around these parts. This lady had some explaining to do.

"No. Not exactly. I'm here in Lone Star Pass because of you," she explained but he was still confused.

"So, let me get this straight. We've never met. You don't know me, but I'm the reason you moved here?" he asked.

"I'm not living here." She shook her head for emphasis. "Just...vacationing for a week or two."

She didn't know how long she was vacationing?

"Sorry, I didn't catch your name," he said, figuring hearing it might ring a bell. She still hadn't come up with an explanation as to where she'd heard his nickname or explained her connection to Bagram.

"Lucas used to talk about you," she said on a sigh, and he noted that she still hadn't willingly given her name. Was she testing him in some strange way? Lucas Hawkins, a.k.a. Hawkeye, was dead and she didn't need to spell out her identity after mentioning him. Based on her prim ballerina silhouette, he knew exactly who she was.

"You must be Catalina Ivey." An IED had caused more

than nerve damage. Twelve months ago, Dane had lost one of his best friends when a roadside explosion created enough confusion for Hawkeye and Bastien to be captured. Hawkeye, had taken point, as usual, on a mission that eventually ended with two fine soldiers going home in pine boxes.

"You know my name?" She sounded confused and more than a little concerned.

"Hawkeye talked about you all the time," Dane admitted. Said she was the love of the man's life and he was going to wear her down and convince him to marry her when his tour was up. This didn't seem like the right time to ask if she'd known about the plan.

"He did?" she asked.

"Yeah." This also didn't seem like the time to tell her soldiers talked to each other, admitting things they normally wouldn't tell a soul, while they were in the dessert.

Dane hadn't thought about Hawkeye in months. He'd suppressed all the memories, good and bad, shoving them down somewhere deep where they wouldn't easily resurface.

"Now that we know who we are—"

"We could catch up over a cup of coffee," Dane cut her off. He wanted to know why she was out here in the middle of nowhere by herself and why she'd chosen Lone Star Pass because of him.

"It's late." There was hesitation in her voice but nothing finite. Inflection was everything and hers said she was on the fence. Did she really want to go back to her cabin alone?

"Or early, depending on your point of view," he said, trying to lighten the mood. His attempt at humor seemed to fall flat.

"Do you know anything about computers?" she finally asked after staring him down for a long moment.

"Afraid not." He put his hands up in the surrender position. "I'm more of a weapons guy than communication."

"Thanks anyway for the coffee offer." She started to walk past him.

"Are you staying at the cabin alone?" His question stopped her in her tracks. Maybe it was the common thread of Hawkeye or the fact the man talked about Catalina endlessly while on missions, and Dane was the unfortunate soul who usually got to listen to how perfect she was or how beautiful. But he didn't want her to leave.

"Maybe. Why do you ask?" She didn't turn to look at him.

"Because I feel like a stranger in my hometown and, frankly, I could use the company." He couldn't see her face clearly enough to decide which way she was leaning. It didn't matter. He shouldn't have asked. It was probably just him missing Hawkeye and feeling all kinds of out of place in Lone Star Pass that had him asking when he should just let her walk away and them both be done with the whole situation.

Her muscles stiffened. Her shoulders came back. Her hands fisted. Dane prepared himself for the blow that would come with rejection as she prepared herself to deliver the punch. Instead, she surprised him by turning around to face him.

"One cup can't hurt," she said, walking toward his cabin.

Rather than pump his fists in the air at the victory, which he wanted to do, he followed her inside. "I probably should have mentioned that I have no idea if there's any coffee here."

She stopped after taking a step inside the door. He flipped on the light, bathing the room in a soft glow.

"Why is that?" she asked.

"The owners don't technically know I'm here," he admitted. "But Jacob is an old friend and I have a standing invite."

His explanation seemed to appease her. She walked over to the adjacent kitchen and went to work, searching for coffee, filters, and cups. Thankfully, all those items were within arm's reach. The layout of the cabins on this row was identical.

"This place is nice," she said, examining a mug. "Why is it your friend doesn't know you're here?" She poured water into the carafe. Her movements were delicate and graceful, belying the tigress she'd been not ten minutes ago who'd dug her fingernails into his arms until they broke the skin.

"This cabin belongs to a friend. I forgot to call and let him know I'd be staying here," he admitted, figuring giving up a little about himself might go a long way toward getting her to relax. Half a dozen questions sprang to mind about the blonde-haired beauty standing in the kitchen, working the coffee machine like she was a barista.

Catalina had a quiet grace and strength. She had the kind of sculpted figure he would imagine on a dancer. Black velvety eyelashes framed the most beautiful cornflower blue eyes. Shoulders straight, chin high, her long neck gave her the elegance of a princess. Her hair could best be described as long, soft, silky blonde waves that fell past her shoulders. It was the kind he'd like to see splayed out across his pillow. A sculptor couldn't have carved better features or created such beauty. Dane stopped himself right there.

Didn't Hawkeye say she was a computer programmer? The profession would make her know a thing or two about needing caffeine to work long hours while staring at a screen. Besides, no good could come from him spending too much time admiring her physical features, perfect as they might be.

The pictures he'd seen of Catalina didn't do her justice. Guilt stabbed at Dane for the attraction he felt toward the woman his buddy had loved.

CATALINA KEPT one eye on Stetson. Even when he thought she'd turned her back on him, she hadn't. Dane Firebrand was a gorgeous man. The photos Lucas had sent home fell woefully short. She'd seen the pictures of him around Lucas and the man was even more attractive in person, if that was even possible. Stetson always stood in the background, though, whereas the other guys crowded the camera phone, throwing an arm around one another or making bunny ears behind someone's head. The photos on one of the most dangerous military bases in the world looked more like an extended high school sleepover than men who faced life and death situations on a daily basis. Looking back, she wondered how much of their posing had been intentional to keep her from worrying about Lucas, her childhood sweetheart, and a love that ran deep.

After pouring two cups, she joined Stetson at the table. Trusting him was another story. Handing one over, their fingers grazed and she ignored the jolt of electricity that came with contact despite the fact it awakened sensations in her she hadn't felt in far too long. Feeling them with one of Lucas's buddies from overseas should make her feel ashamed. So, why didn't they?

"I'm sorry," Stetson said, and she looked into the truest shade of pale blue eyes. He had the thickest, blackest eyelashes framing those gorgeous blues. His hair was black as pitch, on the short side with tight curls. All signs of the military cut was gone, so she assumed he'd been sent somewhere to cool off before the government decided it was a good idea to allow him to interact with civilians again. Aside from that, he was roughly six feet three inches with a body built for sin.

"Thank you." She knew exactly what he referred to... Lucas. "I don't remember seeing you at the..." She flashed eyes at him in an apology.

"No, it's fine." A mix of emotions crossed his expression before he reined them in. Regret? Guilt? A moment of shame? She wasn't trying to make him feel bad for not showing up to the funeral.

"I didn't mean—"

"I couldn't make it. I was in pretty deep overseas and the government didn't think they could trust me to mix with 'regular' people," he admitted.

"Were they right?" She was all too familiar with the policy of finding a place to let soldiers cool off before clearing them for civilian interaction. She'd almost married someone exactly like him.

"Yes." He caught her gaze. Was he searching for disapproval? Disgust? He wouldn't find it with her. She knew better than most what his life had been like overseas. Lucas had shared stories with her that he'd made her swear not to repeat. She'd forced him to open up a little when he'd nearly slit her throat one night when she surprised him in bed. She'd been trying to be playful but quickly learned never to make an unexpected move again when his eyes were closed. He'd changed so much during his time in the military. She'd respected his need to serve but always felt like she lost a little part of him every time he came home, which sometimes wasn't for a year at a time. She suspected he chose not to come home at times when he had leave. Was he afraid she wouldn't approve of the changes in him?

"Why come to Lone Star Pass?" he asked. It was a fair question.

"Lucas mentioned it a few times. He wanted to come here when he got his twenty years in. Buy a little land." The memory was bittersweet.

"And you just decided to rent a cabin here a year after..." Stetson didn't finish the sentence, but it would have been, *after his death.*

"What about you?" She turned the tables. "Why are you slinking around in the middle of the night when your family owns a cattle ranch here? Don't you have a home to go to?"

Stetson issued a sharp sigh. He picked up his cup of coffee and took a sip.

"I guess the answer to your question should be a yes." He tapped his left index finger on the table. "Suffice it to say that I don't exactly want to be seen right now."

"Mind if I ask why?" If she could keep him talking about himself, she might be able to avoid more questions about why she'd come to town.

"Would, 'it's complicated' suffice?" He brought his gaze up to meet hers and the air in the room crackled between them when their eyes met.

Catalina hadn't felt this kind of chemistry before. Ever. There was a lost quality to Stetson's eyes that Catalina connected with on a most basic level. Two broken souls that fit together?

She rejected the idea as unfair to Lucas.

"I'm the last person who is going to try to force you to talk about something you don't want to," she said before taking a sip of the dark brew. It wasn't exactly French roast but was hands down better than tap water.

He shrugged massive shoulders. "My family doesn't exactly get along."

"With all due respect, you're the last person I would expect to shy away from a fight," she said, wishing she could reel those words back in the second they left her mouth after she saw his reaction.

"I'm a work in progress on that one," he said after a few tense moments of silence.

"It's none of my business," she quickly added, grateful for the company. This was the first face-to-face conversation she'd had in twenty days. And looking at Stetson's wasn't exactly a hardship.

"It's fine," he said.

"No, it isn't. I shouldn't poke my nose where it doesn't belong." She shook her head. "I just...it's just been a while since I've really talked to anyone. You know?"

When she lifted her gaze to meet his for the second time, she instantly realized he did know. More than he would probably ever tell. Could she get answers out of him?

3

"You still haven't told me why you're really here." Dane turned the tables, wanting to help if he could.

"I lied before. I'm not on vacation." She took a sip of coffee before setting the mug down and studying it. Her cheeks flushed, making her even more attractive. "Did Lucas tell you what I do for a living?"

"Computer programmer," he said. Catalina was the total package, intelligence and beauty, or so Hawkeye had said more times than Dane could count. Seeing and speaking to her now, Hawkeye hadn't don't her justice.

"Which means I can work anywhere I want," she said. "Within reason."

"Still doesn't explain why you came here," he pointed out.

"That's personal." She shrugged. "Sue me. I miss Lucas. He wanted to move here in a couple of years, so I came here to be close to him."

The explanation didn't sit quite right with Dane. Or maybe it was her expression when she spoke. The way her delicate eyebrow twitched just a little and her cheeks flamed when she mentioned Lucas's name. Something was off.

"So, Stetson, tell me about your family. Will I run into them when I go into town for groceries?" She changed the subject. Another telltale sign she was uncomfortable with the former topic.

"My name out here is Dane," he corrected. His curiosity was piqued because she had no reason to lie to him unless she was doing something illegal. "I left Stetson at Bagram."

"Oh. Right. Sorry." Her cheeks flushed again against creamy skin and he had to fist his hands to keep from reaching out to touch her. He wasn't trying to be a jerk but coming back to civilian life meant he needed to separate himself from his overseas identity. It was the only way he knew how. "Dane."

"It's fine," he said, and he could hear the huskiness in his own voice. Hearing his name roll off her tongue sent an electric impulse rippling through his body from the middle of his chest to his toes.

"You've said that twice now. It's not fine." She lifted her gaze to meet his and his chest took another hit. "Dane it is."

"It's been nice talking to you." He stood up, needing her to go before this attraction got out of control. He immediately regretted his knee-jerk reaction. Being back in Lone Star Pass was getting to him.

A look of surprise darkened her eyes. It seemed to take a second to register that he'd just asked her to leave. Her mouth formed an, "Oh."

Before he could figure out a way to backpedal she was on her feet.

"You didn't willingly tell me your name and you've dodged answering my questions about the real reason you're here," he said, playing these off as the real reasons. There was some truth to what he said. Something wasn't sitting right with what she'd said when they had their first confrontation. "Now that you know I'm not an ax murderer or rapist, you can feel safe to go home."

She stared him down for a long moment like they were playing a game of dare and the loser blinked first. He didn't give an inch.

"Since you already know my name, there's no point in me repeating it. I wasn't lying when I said I was here working. I don't know what else to tell you, but I can take a hint so I'm out of here." She'd skipped over an important detail. He could see it all over her face and he wanted to know what it was. Since asking outright wouldn't get the job done, he'd shocked her in the hopes she'd volunteer information. She wasn't the only one who needed it. He'd had to do the same for himself before a serious attraction could take hold. There was a whole lot of secrecy going on with the beauty inside the cabin, and his familiarity with Hawkeye caused Dane to forget that he didn't know *her*.

His cell buzzed, shocking them both. He fished it out of his pocket as she placed her coffee cup in the sink. He'd noticed that even when it seemed like her back was to him, she kept an eye on him. Good. She shouldn't trust a stranger no matter how comfortable they were. His history with Hawkeye would taint her judgment. Although, Hawk didn't seem to do a whole lot of sharing about his buddies with her.

Jacob's name came up on the screen.

"How do you know where I am?" Dane asked as Catalina crossed the room toward the door.

"You triggered the silent alarm. That's not the reason I called, though," he said. "My folks are on the way there as we speak to spend the week at the cabin so you might want to disappear. Unlucky break."

"That's a shame." Dane needed to find a new place to stay or suck it up and go home. "I'll head out now. They'll never know I was here."

Catalina had stopped.

"Sorry about that, man. Bad timing," Jacob said.

"Not a problem. I can already think of another place to go," Dane reassured.

"Cool. Everything okay?" Jacob asked.

Dane wasn't in the mood for conversation. "I'll take a raincheck on answering that question. Do me a favor?"

"Anything. Name it." Jacob's word was gold.

"Don't tell anyone I was here." Dane watched Catalina, hating the thought she might walk out the door.

"We never talked," Jacob reassured.

Dane thanked his friend before ending the call.

Catalina spun around. "You accused me of being secretive, but you haven't exactly told me why you came home but don't want anyone to know."

"I can't stay here," he said.

"Where will you go?" Concern wrinkled her forehead.

"First, I have to make it seem like I was never here." He shrugged. "Then, maybe I'll grab a couple hours of sleep in my car."

"You can't do that," she countered. "It's too hot outside. You'd have to sleep with the windows open and you'd be eaten alive by mosquitoes. Come next door with me. There's a couch."

"I've slept in much worse conditions and survived," he said. The fact she genuinely seemed to care where he slept touched him.

"Because you had to," she said. "And I have no doubt you

could do it again. The thing is, you'd be punishing yourself for no reason."

"What if I like mosquitoes?" he joked as he made quick work of cleaning up after them, handwashing the mugs and carafe before wiping down the counter and the coffeemaker. When he was done, there was no sign they'd been there.

"Nobody likes mosquitoes," she said, rolling her eyes. "I've insulted you and now you're being difficult."

"Is that right?" He couldn't completely deny her accusation. And since sleeping on a couch seemed a whole lot more comfortable than a sedan, he nodded figuring he could get more information about her and what she was doing in town. His instincts said she was in some kind of trouble. Dane wanted to help. *For Hawkeye.*

"Prove me wrong. Say you'll stay over." The look she shot him next made it clear she was issuing a dare. Her balled fist on her hip pushed him over the edge. Then, she dropped her hand and softened her stance. "If not for me, do it for Lucas. He would want me to make the offer."

Now, he couldn't refuse.

"I'll stay," he said.

"Good," she stated. The defiance in her eyes said she was having an internal battle. He intended to find out what she was hiding.

CATALINA WALKED in front of Dane. She was all of five feet four inches so the man had almost a foot of height on her. At least part of her wanted to explain her situation to him, see if he would understand. It couldn't hurt to have someone to bounce ideas off of. Lucas had respected this man and trusted him with his life. Could she risk it?

Expose herself and what she was doing and she could incriminate herself. As it was, she only had her word against her boss on the conversation she'd overheard. Besides, no District Attorney would file a case based on hearsay. She needed proof. She needed to finish the app she was working on and sell it to a competitor. Hanson Tech would do the right thing with it. No question there. As for her non-compete clause—the clause every tech person signed with an employer that said they wouldn't develop software and then sell it to a competitor or leave to work for them—Hanson Tech would be able to get her out of that as well. On balance, she decided there was too much on the line to tell anyone what she was doing no matter how connected she felt to Dane. She chalked her familiarity up to his connection to Lucas.

"Home sweet home," she said, unlocking the door to the cabin before opening it.

He signaled for her to go first, and he reached over to hold the door for her. Turned out chivalry wasn't dead. Catalina appreciated the gesture. It showed the rancher-turned-Spec-Ops-soldier's manners—manners she wished more people embraced.

The cabin she rented had the same layout but that's where the similarities ended. This one had updated wood flooring, cream-colored paint, and comfy oversized furniture in warm tones. There were peaceful pictures of bridges covering the walls and a water fountain was on most of the time in the kitchen. The serenity of the place had attracted her.

She used her body to block Dane's view of her opened laptop. The toothless angel on the screensaver would give away more information than she was ready to share. The biggest question came an instant later...could she trust him at all?

Catalina absently fingered the chain of the dog tags she kept with her at all times. When she felt especially alone, she wore them.

"What kind of project are you working on?" Dane's voice cut through her thoughts.

She cleared her throat and motioned toward the sofa, closing her laptop before he could get a good look. "It's a tracking app used for scalping." A quick glance at a confused Dane brought a smile out. She took a seat across the coffee table from him and then hugged a pillow against her chest.

"Is this like buying concert tickets?" His eyebrow came up.

"The app will track digital goods. At least that's what it's supposed to do. It isn't much of anything right now." She exhaled long and slow, resisting the urge to pinch the bridge of her nose to stave off the stress headache trying to take shape. Her blurry eyes burned from staring at a screen too many hours in the day. Bottom line? The faster she finished this program, the quicker she got to hold her baby again. Dry eyes would be more than worth the sacrifice if she could pull this off. Catalina refused to consider the possibility she couldn't. She also needed to find proof of what Kal Sutton actually planned to do with her app, once the developmental stage was finished.

"Sounds like an app like the one you mentioned will be worth a lot," Dane said.

She nodded and then realized she'd forgotten her manners completely. "Would you like something to drink?"

"I barely took two sips of coffee at Jacob's place. You have any here?" he asked.

"Of course." She set the pillow down and pushed to standing. "I have cream and sugar if you'd like."

"Black is good for me," he said. "But can I help? I'd hate to force you to make coffee twice in the same hour."

"It's no trouble." She waved him off. Besides, having him here felt strangely intimate. She hadn't been alone with a man besides Lucas in a very long time. Putting on a fresh pot would give her something to do with her hands while she gained control over an attraction she had no idea what to do with.

"Who would buy an app like this?" Dane asked, leaning forward, hands clasped with his elbows on his thighs. The man was clearly uncomfortable relaxing.

"A lot of people. So, I need to make one hundred percent certain it falls into the right hands," she said.

"I thought you worked for a government contractor," Dane said. He really did know more about her than she realized. She was also at a disadvantage because he was a mystery. Lucas only briefly discussed his friends on the rare occasions he came home to Ardmore, Oklahoma, where they both grew up with their families.

"Right now, I'm doing a freelance project." She figured it was true enough. The idea of lying didn't sit well. She'd always been terrible at misleading people. It was half the reason she'd known she had to leave Tech Corp after over-hearing her boss; one look and she would have given herself away.

"What would you think if I told you my scalping app was going to be paired with a GPS program. Where would your mind snap to?" She finished making the coffee and brought over twin mugs, which she set on the glass table. No way was she risking their fingers touching again while she was feeling so vulnerable.

"I'd wonder why you needed a GPS component for a tracking app in the first place. What you said a minute ago was that your app only tracks digital goods. So, that's an online trail. GPS would allow for a physical component." He thanked her for the fresh brew, picked up the mug and took a sip. "Now that's coffee."

"French roast." She shrugged. "What can I say, I'm spoiled over here."

"Why are you asking me the question, by the way?" he asked. Dane might not be a computer guru, but the man seemed like a quick study.

"Because this combined product is supposed to be sold to the US government. I got excited when I first realized the implication." She lowered her gaze because she couldn't look at Dane when she said the next words. "This could help someone like my Lucas. The government could have tracked his location after he was captured. Maybe things would have turned out differently."

"That's a dangerous product in the wrong hands," Dane said after a thoughtful pause.

"It sure is," she confirmed.

When she looked up, she could practically see the wheels turning in Dane's mind, connecting dots. And she wondered if she'd just made a critical mistake.

4

"This app would be worth a fortune, right?" Dane asked, wondering if she'd left her job to develop this on her own and sell it to the highest bidder. From everything Lucas had said about her, there was no way she would do anything illegal or immoral. After meeting her, Dane would have to agree. He'd always been a decent judge of character and hers struck him as honest and responsible.

But he also wanted to know why she was out here in a small Texas town renting a fishing cabin while working on a secret project. Then there was the fear in her eyes during their first encounter. The way she fought back like it meant her life was on the line. Dots were connecting in his mind.

"The answer to your question is yes," she admitted. "But this isn't what you think."

"How do you know what's going on in my head?" he asked. The last thing he wanted to do was spook her even more. She seemed like she was in some kind of trouble. Maybe with her former boss. Maybe with the government.

He'd bet his life savings she didn't book this rental under her real name.

"Because it's the first place mine would go to if I were in your shoes." She picked up her mug and started to take a drink but stopped short of letting the rim touch her lips— lips he didn't need to notice the fullness of or their rich pink color. "And you'd be right. I'm here because I overheard my boss in a conversation that made me believe he is in league with the wrong government. So, I factory reset my work computer and did the same with my company issued laptop. I always have my own, so that's the one I'm traveling with because I can't risk getting caught until I have proof of what my boss planned to do with the app. Mine was supposed to be a scalping app. There was never supposed to be a GPS component."

"You don't have proof, or you would have come forward." He put two and two together. If there was an app that could track military personnel's location and information, and then execute, this would be critical to retrieving POWs. After losing Lucas, she would go all-in for a program like this. But Dane saw the darker side immediately. He didn't need to overhear a conversation to realize this would be awful for soldiers. Besides, there were places operatives had to go while on a mission that was no one's business.

"I also need the money from the sale of this app since I no longer have a job," she admitted. She tucked her feet underneath her bottom and hugged the pillow to her chest. Lucky pillow.

"You don't strike me as the greedy type, so you're going to have to explain to me why you want to finish the program and sell it." He couldn't think of one good reason for her to follow through with coding on the app.

She swallowed. Hard. Her pulse pounded at the base of

her neck. She was about to reveal something he wasn't so sure he wanted to know about her.

"First of all, Lucas was taken as a prisoner of war before being tortured and killed, and his body shipped back in a box to our hometown of Oklahoma, so I don't take this lightly and I won't betray his memory by making it easier on the other side to do the same with other soldiers. The company I worked for has some military contracts. We were freelancers and also developed software for regular companies." Her voice shook, giving away her emotions, but make no mistake about it, this lady was strong. "If I can finish my side of the app, I can sell it to a competitor. I know exactly who."

"Why sell it at all?" he asked.

"Because I have a child to think about." She practically glared at him. "And, yes, my son belongs to Lucas."

This information was the equivalent of a bomb detonating in Dane's brain.

"Lucas never said anything about a pregnancy or child," Dane said, still trying to process why Lucas would keep the information from his brothers in arms. The answer came almost instantly. He wouldn't. "He didn't know?"

"And it's better that way," she said.

"How so? Because last time I checked, he had a right to know he had a child." Dane's defensiveness was misplaced. He couldn't separate how he would feel if this news was dropped in his lap and knew Lucas would have the same mindset.

She shook her head. Despite her strong front, a tear rolled down her cheek. "I would have told him but I didn't find out I was pregnant until after he went missing. And you know how I found out that happened? His mother called. Lucas and I weren't married. We didn't live together. So, the military informed his mother and I found out secondhand. When I called her to tell her about the pregnancy she said I was lying and hung up on me."

Dane could see the pain in her eyes. She ducked her head, chin to chest, and coughed. He figured the move was meant to stop her from full-on crying. Talking about their child would only make it worse, so he gave her an out.

"What about a non-compete? Don't you have to sign something when you go to work for a company that says you won't develop something and then turn around and sell it to a competitor?" he asked.

"The company I'm targeting is twice as big and their lawyers are twice as smart. They'll know how to protect me," she said. "Tech Corp won't have a chance. But right now, all I have is an overheard conversation. I can point a finger but haven't found the proof. And, if Kal finds me before I finish this program and have any sort of bargaining chip, it's game over."

"Not while I'm here," he stated.

"What?" she asked. The shock in her voice only matched by the expression in her blue eyes.

"I'd like to help," he said. "I failed Lucas in life, Catalina. I don't want to fail him in death."

"Don't you have a family obligation?" Her brows drew together as she rolled the mug in between her hands. His words clearly struck a chord.

"It can wait," he stated, but she was already shaking her head.

"I can't let you do this," she said.

"Why not?" He needed to hear her objections so he could make her see reason.

"It's dangerous, for one." She glanced over at him and must've realized what she'd just said. "I do realize you've just come from a hot zone. This might be a trigger for you."

"I've already cooled off," he pointed out. "The military never would have released me if they didn't think I could handle it."

She shot him another look that called him out.

"Okay," he said. "There are ways to get past the system. Except that I was in no hurry to leave the former Virginia tobacco farm to see my family, so you can trust that I didn't pull any tricks."

Catalina seemed to think long and hard about her next words.

"I appreciate your offer of help, Dane. I really do. But—"

"No arguing. I want to do this, Catalina. Let me help. It's the least I can do for an old friend." It didn't matter that Dane and Lucas weren't as close as some of the other guys. But then Dane didn't get 'close' with anyone. People were best kept at arm's length. So, why did his heart want to get close to Catalina?

THE VERY LAST thing Catalina should be doing was refusing help.

Dane picked up his coffee mug and his hand started shaking. He immediately switched hands, narrowly saving her the cleanup of black coffee on a cream-colored area rug. But that wasn't the point. She watched as he flexed his hand a few times and her heart went out to him.

"First of all, thank you for your service," she said, choking back more tears, refusing to let them fall.

"You're welcome," Dane said mechanically, like he'd said it a hundred times before. He most likely had and, based on what Lucas had told her, it never got old. But he was distracted and trying to convince her of something she wasn't so certain was a good idea.

"And secondly, I don't want to keep you from your family. If anything, this whole ordeal has reminded me how important family is," she began, searching for the right words.

"Mine does nothing but argue," he said. He managed a sip of coffee, holding the bottom of the cup with his left hand.

"Can I ask how long you were in the military?" She figured he might not answer but it didn't hurt to ask.

"Seventeen years," he admitted.

"You were so close to twenty," she said quietly, realizing that meant he most likely medically boarded out.

"But I didn't make it and it's fine," he said.

The minute he'd used the word "fine," she knew the opposite was true.

"You were planning on a career," she stated.

"Plans change," he said. He had a ready answer for everything, it seemed.

She didn't want to step on toes but if she was going to consider letting him help her, she wanted to know something about him.

"For what it's worth, I'm sorry," she said quietly.

An emotion passed behind those true blues of his. Regret? Anger? Frustration? A mix of all three? Pinpointing it didn't seem to matter to her heart. It still broke anyway.

"Last time I checked you weren't there." He winked and she figured it was meant to be playful. Was this how he deflected when he didn't want to deal with something?

She took note. Lucas had so many coping mechanisms. It seemed he had a quick line for almost anything she said, forget serious conversation. He turned most heavy conversations into a joke or a reason to be intimate. He'd dodged giving real answers and she let him.

"You're right. But I am here. And if I'm going to accept your help, I want to know something more about you." Her comment was rewarded with a show of perfectly straight, white teeth when he smiled. He had the kind of smile that caused her pulse to kick up a few notches and her breath to quicken.

Rather than give away her reaction to him, she took another sip of coffee and curled her legs tighter around her bottom.

"You mentioned your family. Do you have siblings?" She figured the question was safe and a good place to start.

He laughed and his eyes lit up.

"You could say I have a few siblings," he stated. "Or maybe a few more than that."

Well, now she really was curious. "Am I supposed to guess? Three? Four?"

"Not even close. Eight siblings to be exact. All boys," he said much to her astonishment. Her brain couldn't begin to process going through pregnancy after pregnancy let alone the birthing process with nine kids.

"I can't imagine the amount of laundry that went on in your house." She blinked a couple of times at the thought. Luke was a baby and it felt like she had to constantly throw in a load. "And all of you have the same parents? No modern family blending?"

"There are nine sons on my side of the family and nine more on my uncle's side," he said.

"All guys?" What were the odds of that happening?

"Yes. One set of twin cousins." He seemed to be enjoying her shock.

"Forget about laundry. I can't imagine your parents' grocery bill." She could only imagine how poor they must have been. She pictured a life of hand-me-downs. The first few weeks of Luke's life all she did was change his diaper and feed him. His formula equaled the price of gold.

He really laughed now.

"What's so funny?" She didn't bother to hide the defensiveness in her tone.

"You clearly haven't heard of the last name Firebrand," was all he said.

If she'd brought anything but a throw-away phone she'd look it up right then and there. "Wait a second. Why does that name ring a bell?" She snapped her fingers. "Something about cattle?"

"A little something," he teased, clearly having a good time at her expense. The spark in his eyes only made him more appealing.

"Tell me what that means or I'll get up and look your family up on my laptop right now." She wasn't falling into the trap of wanting something she could never have.

"My family is one of the wealthiest in Texas." He retrieved his cell from his back pocket, pulled up a search engine, and typed in his name. He had to stop twice to pump his right hand like he'd lost feeling and was trying to get it back. Nerve damage?

He handed over the phone and she stared at the screen.

"Not one of...*the*," she stated. It didn't make any sense. Why risk his life overseas when he could be sitting pretty on his family's ranch?

"You're overthinking this," came the calm voice. "I can tell by the wrinkle in your forehead."

Her cheeks flushed at the fact he'd noticed one of her quirks. "I'm just surprised. That's all."

"Wondering why a rich kid like me would go looking for trouble in another country?" he asked.

"I wouldn't put it that way," she corrected. "It's honorable that you wanted to serve your country. But let's face it. You don't need the pension."

"Oh yeah? What makes you think I want to lean on my family for my income? I'd rather make my own way in life," he said. There was no hint of anger in his voice. He stated facts, like he was reading nutritional content off a cereal box when he talked about finances. The topic of his family was another story altogether. His eyes darkened, his lips thinned, hinting at a deeper story to be told there.

"It's a shame," she said. "I'd fallen into the trap of thinking money could solve all problems."

"You're not alone," he quickly said.

"If money isn't the magic bullet, then I wonder what is?" She was thinking out loud more so than expecting an answer. Because she, for one, could attest to the fact lack of money didn't exactly breed happiness. She'd grown up with very little but managed to put herself through school, get a degree, and then a decent job. Two years of community college before transferring to UT Dallas to finish her bachelor's, which had taken another four while waitressing the early morning shift at a popular Brazilian breakfast haunt near campus. Working her way through school hadn't been easy or quick but doing it on her own gave her a real sense of pride. Maybe she could understand his need for independence more than she realized. There was another connection to him she didn't want to acknowledge or admit.

A deep-seeded place that made her want to depend on no one but herself. Could she let someone else in?

5

"If you figure out the secret, let us all in on it." Dane had no clue. All he knew for certain was that money didn't solve all life's problems.

Catalina bit back a yawn as she nodded.

"Am I keeping you awake?" Dane asked, thinking she looked a little too tempting with those sparkly eyes. So much so, thoughts of them both in bed, limbs intertwined, assaulted him.

"Not really," she said. "I took a nap a couple of hours ago. I've been churning on this code too long. Taking a step away for a little while is actually my best chance to find a solution."

"Does anyone else know what you were working on when you walked off your job?" Dane asked.

"Blaine Rockwell. He's the one who was writing the GPS code. I don't know if he realized what it was truly for, though," she admitted.

"What about your competitor?" He took a sip of coffee. He did his best thinking in the middle of the night but realized not everyone was a night owl like him. The military might have trained him to wake up early, but it had never quite seeded. The minute he went on leave, he reverted back. Another not so fun fact was that cattle ranchers woke before the sun. Yet another reason Dane had never quite fit with the rest of his family.

"Did Hanson know? Anything is possible, but I don't believe he would care one way or the other about what Tech Corp was doing," she said. "Other than from a purely competitive standpoint. I doubt they would know what Kal intended to do with an app like the one I'm developing."

"Are you sure about that? Corporate spying isn't new and those government contracts mean big money," he said. "I never trust anyone in business who deals with millions of dollars like they were handing out change."

"That is a really good point." She hugged the pillow tighter and then pinched the corner seam between her thumb and forefinger. A nervous tic?

"We could do a little digging into the CEO's background. See if anything comes up," he said.

"I can do better than that. I can hack into his cell phone and see what his communication looks like when he thinks it's secure," she said.

"You can do that?" he asked.

She shot him a look. "With enough time, I can hack into most pieces of technology. I'd go in through his e-mail since it'll be linked with his phone. Most CEOs use their cell more than a laptop."

"There's only one problem." He hesitated to point out the obvious but it needed to be said. She needed to continue grinding the code to create the app in the first place. He didn't have any computer skills, hacking or otherwise. And now that he knew she had a child in the wings, time was even more of the essence. "You're going to be busy enough already without adding to your workload."

"And there's only one of me," she agreed. "It would take time I don't have and may not give the answers I'm looking for."

"Prioritizing your time is the most important thing right now," he said.

She nodded.

"Where's your son?" He held up a hand before she could answer. "Never mind. You should keep that information on a need-to-know basis."

Again, she nodded.

"I can cover you from a security standpoint, so you don't have to split your focus." He could keep watch and make sure she had enough food to keep going. She could bounce ideas off him. Although, to be fair, he wouldn't have the first idea what she was really saying when it came to coding. Still, it might help to have a sounding board.

She studied him for a long moment.

"What are you really saying here, Dane?" she finally asked.

"That'd I'd like to help, if you'll allow it." He couldn't state his intention any more directly than that. She needed someone to keep watch over her while she focused. His intentions were purely platonic despite the pull of attraction he felt.

"Why would you do that?" Her arched brow said she either couldn't believe he would be willing to set aside his own life for hers or she didn't trust him to get the job done.

"Because I can," he stated simply.

"Doesn't really answer my question," she said.

He leaned back in his chair and caught her gaze, wondering how much he wanted to share about what was going on inside his head. "Do you have any regrets in life? Anything you wished like anything you could go back in time for ten seconds and change?"

"Generally speaking, I don't do regrets," she said.

"Why is that?" he wondered out loud.

"They're a waste of time and energy." She picked up her mug and took a sip of coffee but never took her eyes off him. "And they don't change a thing. I try to look at them as lessons and move on. If I learned from a mistake, I can't regret it, right?"

"Normally, I'd agree with you one hundred percent," he said.

"And now?" she asked.

"I'm more ninety-five percent." He stretched his legs out, crossing them at the ankles. The move would make it difficult to stand up quickly, therefore making him less physically intimidating, and should put her more at ease. She might not realize all that was going on in her subconscious, but him being less of a threat to her would resonate somewhere in the back of her mind. The place that told her when to tense for a fight and when to relax. If he could get her to relax around him, she would be more likely to accept his help.

"What happened to the five percent?" she continued, leaning forward, curious.

"The day Lucas was captured. I'd go back to that day and tell him not to be the one to volunteer point. I'd raise my hand instead and refuse to take no for an answer because he would argue about it. There's a reason we called him Hawkeye and it wasn't just because of his last name. He was a damn fine soldier and nothing got past him." Dane stopped right there. He refused to say the rest to Lucas's widow. The two might not have been legally married but they'd been family nonetheless. The piece of paper was only a formality in his book now that he'd learned about Lucas's son.

"What was different that time out, if you don't mind my asking?" Her voice was barely a whisper and there was still so much pain, even a year later.

"Everything and nothing. We did everything the same way we always did. I'd blame bad intel but there was more to it than that. Violence had been escalating in the area. Communication felt 'off' that day." He shrugged but the day had replayed in his mind dozens of times since. He'd had nightmares. The kind that woke him in a cold sweat.

Dane never talked about that day. Not with anyone. A coil tightened in his chest now, threatening to spring, break through bone, and send rib fragments flying everywhere. This seemed like a good time to remind himself Catalina deserved to know what happened.

He took in a sharp breath and continued. "People talk about getting bad feelings. Premonitions. We all had to learn to ignore our instincts and trust the intel, our training. Every one of us in the unit became experts at it. It's how we survived and continued to do our jobs." He paused long enough to polish off his coffee before setting the empty mug on the coffee table. "It's like instincts have a shut-off valve and we had to find it during basic or there was no point in signing up for the job."

"Lucas talked about it with me once when he was trying to explain the changes in him." She dropped her gaze to the pillow, still working the corner in between her thumb and forefinger. "Over the years he seemed to get better and better at shutting down his emotions. I asked him why. He used similar words. Said his survival depended on it at work."

"A career soldier gets really good at it. It's the only way to do our job," he said.

Catalina set the pillow to one side, stood up, and walked around the coffee table. She sat beside him on the couch, and then placed her hand on top of his. The electrical current running through his veins caused a jolt that made his whole future play out in front of him—a future he didn't deserve because it should be Lucas's.

He cleared his throat and jerked his hand out from underneath hers, half expecting her to withdraw or show signs of embarrassment.

When she didn't, a bomb detonated inside his chest. One he couldn't afford. "You should go back to the other couch."

~

"And if I don't?" Catalina challenged Dane with her stare. There was no way she was backing down like she had with Lucas, leaving her with the nagging feeling she could have done more. Year after year, she'd watched him become less of what made him Lucas. His compassion slipped away, like shower water in a tub drain, slowly cycling out until there wasn't much more left than a shell.

Without compassion, what did anyone truly have?

"Free country," he said angrily, but she also heard the huskiness in his voice. Were his walls threatening to crack?

When she'd pushed the issue with Lucas once, he'd blown up at her and told her that she shouldn't expect him to be something he wasn't anymore. She could deal with the new him or hit the door. The old Lucas never would have issued an ultimatum. But then again, he'd seen, heard, and done things that would have to change a person. The evidence had been everywhere and she'd been so blind. Part of her had expected the old Lucas to come back once he retired and got some time away from the job. Time to be normal again. She'd started counting down the days. And despite falling out of love with him a very long time ago, she refused to walk away from the only man she'd ever truly cared about.

Looking back, loving Lucas had become more habit than anything else. She'd loved him when they were in middle school. Loved him during high school. Loved him all throughout college. And it frustrated her to no end that she couldn't love him enough to bring him back from the dark emotional place he'd gone.

"Is it?" she asked, knowing full well there were too many men and women who'd paid the ultimate price for everyone else's freedom.

"It better be," came the response. "Or everything we went through is for nothing."

She nodded and stayed by his side. He stood up and paced, raking his fingers through his dark as pitch hair.

Catalina stood up too. She moved to the kitchen where she poured a glass of water, aware of Dane's every move as heat came off him in palpable waves. This time, she couldn't stand idly by when she might be able to help.

"Talk to me," she said softly.

Dane whirled around to face her, his gaze the equivalent of a lion staring down its prey. A moment of fear rocketed through her. She couldn't stop herself from trembling just a little despite believing in her heart of hearts that he would never do anything to hurt her intentionally.

Then, he crossed the room in a couple of quick strides. She turned to follow him with her gaze, her backside pressed against the bullnose granite edge countertop. Dane ate up the real estate between them and then positioned his hands on either side of her, grabbing hold of the granite, essentially trapping her. Catalina had two choices, duck out of the box he created around her or stand there and face him down.

For a split second, self-preservation kicked in, begging her to duck and then get as far away from this man as possible. Giving in felt like a failure. Could she live with herself if she failed twice?

Catalina dug her heels in. She refused to give an inch despite the intensity of Dane's stare, his threatening presence, or the fact she couldn't think clearly when he filled her senses with his outdoorsy, spicy scent.

"Tell me what's going on in your mind," she said, making eye contact and staying the course. If only she'd been so brave with Lucas, would he have drifted so far away from her? Would he have gone to that dark place that caused him to drink a little too much when he was home? Would he still be alive today? Able to hold his son? Able to tell her what she should do because she was new to this whole mom business and pretty sure she was messing it up at every turn.

"Why do you care?" came out through clenched teeth.

"Why wouldn't I?" she shot back.

"You don't know me," he practically growled.

"You're right." She risked touching his hands.

This time, he didn't jerk his away. She could feel a tremor in his right hand and wanted to know how he got it. It couldn't have been that day. Did it just happen? Another trauma? After losing two men in his unit—men he cared about—had he kept going until he'd become the target?

"Tell me who you are, Dane Firebrand," she said, not budging an inch no matter how much her heart pounded the base of her throat at staring into the pain in those pure blue eyes. "I want to help."

He stood there for a long moment and it seemed like time stood still. He stared into her eyes like he was trying to read her. Maybe even decide if he could open up to her. And then he blinked, a wall came up, and she saw nothing relatable in his gaze.

"Thanks for the offer, sweetheart. But I'm not the chatty type. I'll pass." With that, he smirked before taking a step back. He retrieved his coffee cup and moved to the sink next to her like nothing had just happened.

Her heart sank in her chest, frustration burned, and she was filled with an emptiness that caused a physical ache. And just like that, she was back at that place and in that moment when she'd found out Lucas wasn't ever coming home. In a word...helpless.

Digging deep, pulling from all her strength, Catalina refused to let her knees buckle.

"Are you a coward?" she said to the back of his head. The comment stopped him in his tracks. He fisted the hands at his sides. For a split second, she believed he might just turn around and unleash hell on her.

He didn't.

Instead, Dane turned his head to the side just enough for her to watch his mouth move when he spoke. He barely gave her a glance when he said, "No. But I am broken. And sweetheart, not even you can fix me."

"I don't accept that." Catalina had no idea where this bravado was coming from except that she'd lost enough already. "It's an excuse and we both know it."

His smirk returned.

"You don't let up, do you?" he asked.

"I did once and it cost me someone I cared deeply about.

Promised myself that I'd never do it again if I had another chance." The admission put her out of her comfort zone. But then, this whole conversation qualified.

"Let me help you out here," he said. "You can't save me."

Why did those words from a practical stranger make her want to curl up in the fetal position and cry?

6

"Mind if I give you a piece of advice?"

Catalina shrugged. Her shoulders rounded forward and her lips curled into a frown, causing Dane to feel like a real jerk.

"Go ahead," she said.

"Whatever Lucas did, said, or didn't do...forgive him." It was as simple and complicated as that. Trying to fix Dane wouldn't change how she felt about what happened with Lucas.

"I already have," she said. Her chin quivered despite holding her head high when she said the words. He believed she meant them, which meant something else caused her to want to 'fix' Dane.

"I'll take you up on your offer of help," she said. "But no more discussions about my relationship with Lucas."

"Okay then." Dane realized he'd struck a raw nerve. Had she truly forgiven Lucas for his mistakes? For all his short-comings? For his temper? Trying to have a 'normal' relationship back home while doing the things required of a soldier didn't mesh. It required a person to split themselves in two in order to do it successfully. Dane had seen the casualties, the broken promises, the frustrated girlfriends and wives. Only a psychopath devoid of true emotion could slip in and out of the two roles without leaving collateral damage.

It was the primary reason Dane kept his relationships casual. No strings attached. No expectations on either side. He was upfront and his partners knew exactly what they were getting into straight out of the gate. Great sex. No sticky emotions. They could do as they pleased. His only request was that they both be monogamous for as long as they were hooking up.

The sun brightened the eastern horizon, peeking through the slats in the kitchen window mini blinds. Their conversation had left him edgy and her tense. He could think of an interesting way to relieve their tension, but sex with Catalina could never be a one-time thing, and he highly doubted she'd be willing to play by his rules.

"Do you want to grab a few hours of shut-eye before getting started today?" he asked, figuring he could keep watch for a few hours.

"I'd rather bring you up to speed on what I've been doing the past three weeks, where I've been, and what you should be looking out for." She stood there, hip leaning against the counter a few feet away from him. Her arms were crossed over her chest and she refused to make eye contact.

"Talk," he said, moving toward the fridge. "I'll make breakfast."

"I haven't spent more than one week in a place since leaving the office twenty-one days ago. The shortest record is three days. Austin. And I probably shouldn't have gone there in the first place because Kal already knows it's one of my favorite cities. I feel like there's always someone just one step behind me, but I might just be paranoid at this point." She dropped her arms to her sides, palms out, an improvement in her body language. "It's been a very real couple of weeks and I feel like I'm living out some thriller movie instead of my life."

Dane nodded as he pulled out a carton of eggs. There was lunch meat and cheese, so he pulled those out too. On the counter, he'd seen a bag of bagels. He could work with these ingredients. Two bagels went in the toaster while he fried a pair of eggs.

"I'm close to finishing the code but I need another week. I'd take a few uninterrupted days, though, to be honest. Beggars can't be choosers," she continued while he worked.

"Have you seen anyone follow you or is it just a feeling? Like eyes watching you?" The distinction was important and would tell him how much of this was her imagination getting the best of her or real fact.

"I could have sworn I saw the same guy in Austin as I did in Tulsa. He's always wearing dark glasses and a black cowboy hat," she said.

"No one wears a black hat in the middle of summer," he stated.

"I know. It's the reason he stood out to me." Her eyes lit up and he forced his gaze back to the breakfast bagel he was building.

He built the layers, bagel on bottom, then a slice of cheese. Ham was next and then came the fried egg. He made a move to open a cabinet in front of him, but she shook her head and opened the one nearest her. She pulled out two plates and set them down. One by one, he scooped his creation onto them.

"I have to say, I'm impressed," Catalina said, causing him to smile despite their heavy exchange a few minutes ago.

"They taste even better than they look," he said, drumming up a casual tone, trying to lighten the mood.

She stared at him for a long moment and he could almost predict the questions forming. Why did a wealthy cattle ranch kid know how to cook? How had he honed his kitchen skills in the military?

His own mother was an incredible cook. He'd picked up a few ideas watching her. But mostly, Catalina would probably be surprised to learn how much he'd learned to depend on himself growing up in a family with nine kids.

Setting the plates on the table, he poured himself another cup of coffee. He held up the pot. "Do you want a refill?"

"No, thanks. I like my morning caffeine cold." She pulled a Coke from the fridge before sitting down at the table made for four. The furniture in this cabin was a helluva lot more comfortable than Jacob's but it also took up more room, making the place cozier. The décor was neutral with more feminine touches. Salt and pepper shakers in the form of spring flowers. A variety of pale pinks and purples in the form of throw pillows and place settings.

Dane took his seat, having to remind himself this was no date, despite the fact he hadn't sat down for a meal with someone from the opposite sex in years. This mirrored a real date, unlike the 'get togethers' he'd orchestrated which might involve food at some point but was normally an order take-out and eat in bed situation. He found taking this tact led to less confusion in the long run.

"The guy with the hat. What else did you notice?" He needed to steer the conversation back on track. Keep focused.

She took a bite of the sandwich and a little moan of

pleasure escaped. Wasn't exactly good for the whole 'keeping focused' angle.

"He was tall, but not like you," she said in between bites. The way she wolfed down her food made him think she hadn't had a good meal in days. "More like Lucas's height."

"A hair under six feet," he said, and she nodded. "What about his build?"

"He looked more like a runner than a bodybuilder." She glanced up and to the left, a sure sign of recalling facts. "He had on jeans and a black t-shirt, which stuck out in Austin. You know?"

He did know. The city was overrun with eighteen to twenty-two year-olds considering the University of Texas's main campus was smack in the middle of town. It was a sea of backpacks and burnt orange apparel. "Someone dressed like that would stand out."

He noticed her navy blue quilted backpack tucked up against the sofa and figured despite being in her thirties she could fit right in with the college crowd. Especially when he considered the number of grad students in the mix.

Dane took a bite of his breakfast and chewed.

"There are all kinds of people downtown, but none of them caught my eye in the way he did," she said. "Plus, he kept watching me like he was trying not to."

"There are other explanations as to why a man might watch an attractive woman," he said. "None of them have to do with corporate espionage or stalking."

She kept her gaze on her food as she took another bite. The fact she didn't, or couldn't, make eye contact meant she was uncomfortable with a compliment. Duly noted. The last thing he wanted to do was make her uncomfortable around him. He also noticed how quickly she cleaned her plate. Her cheeks flushed as though his comment embarrassed her. Did she not realize how incredibly beautiful she was?

"I BETTER GET BACK TO IT." Catalina needed to deflect attention because the red blush crawling up her neck had reached her cheeks. She stood up and collected her plate and silverware. "I'll do dishes since you cooked."

Dane shook his head. "No dice. You have one job right now and you promised to let me handle the rest."

Catalina couldn't remember the last time someone took care of her. Even in her relationship with Lucas, she'd carried most of the weight. And Dane made a good point. Coding was her priority. She nodded before moving to the couch, picking up her laptop along the way. She settled in, thinking how easy it had been to slip into the role of taking care of Lucas. In the rare times he came home she took time off work, dropped everything, and did her best to make up for lost time. It was silly, looking back, how she'd begun to feel the pressure of keeping the relationship going on her shoulders without expecting much in return.

Lucas loved her in the best way he knew how. But should she have expected more? She was a strong person, but every once in a while she'd wished there was someone who could hug her and make her believe everything would work out.

The screensaver on her laptop made her smile, realizing a piece of Lucas would always be with her in their child. The thought of bringing up Luke alone scared her. Forget the red cape, single parents were her new superheroes.

Fingers on the keyboard, she glanced over at Dane, who was whistling. The fact he was self-sufficient, well, grateful didn't nearly express how she felt about his presence. Finding out he came from one of the wealthiest cattle ranching families had thrown her for a loop, though. For one, he didn't act like someone who had money. He was dressed in normal clothes, served his country in the military, and had a down-to-earth quality despite being one of the sexiest men she'd ever seen. She couldn't help but wonder what else she didn't know about the mysterious man—a man who'd been close to Luke's father.

She bit back a yawn, wishing her Coke would kick in already. Then again, she hadn't slept more than a nap here and there in the past fifty-two hours, a personal record. Giving birth five months ago had definitely taken away some of her ability to crush late nights and work long stretches. Speaking of which, she extended her arms as far as they would go to get the blood moving again, and bit back another yawn. Curiosity got the best of her so she Googled Dane's name.

The information from her search was a shot of caffeine to the system if ever there was one. Hearing Dane was from a rich family was one thing. Seeing their sprawling home and aerial views of the ranch was another. Then, there were all the charities his mother supported. His grandfather looked like an unhappy soul. She scrolled through the multitude of images and society stories.

When she looked up, Dane was standing right beside her. She gasped and quickly closed the laptop.

"If you want to know something about me...ask. I'm right here." There was no amusement in his voice.

"Sorry, I was curious. I guess. Surfing for a few minutes usually helps me shift gears before I go into deep concentration mode. I was too embarrassed to ask how big your family home is or what your life is like on the ranch." The admission caused her cheeks to burn. "I'll just open this and click off."

"What does it say?" he asked.

"Basically? Your family is loaded," she said matter-of-fact. "In a league all of your own."

"That pretty much sums it up," he said. "But ranchers aren't in it for the show."

"I figured that out after talking to you for five minutes. Don't take this the wrong way but you're one of the most down-to-earth people I've ever met," she said. "And I mean that as a compliment."

Risking a glance, she couldn't help but notice the smirk on his face. "What?"

"I've been called a lot of things in my day by the opposite sex. That's a first," he said.

"What can I say? I'm an original," she stated. With him standing this close, heat pinged between them. Heat she couldn't afford to feel for half a dozen reasons, not the least of which was the fact that Dane had served with Lucas. She was certain there was an unspoken rule against wondering what his thick lips would feel like against hers. Or, better yet, feathering kisses down her neck.

Catalina tried to physically shake off the thought.

"Everything okay?" he asked, one of his dark brows arched.

"My eyes are blurring and I can't seem to stop yawning. My brain can't seem to focus despite the caffeine, either," she admitted.

"How long since you've slept more than a nap here and there?" he asked.

"A couple of days." She patted her stomach. "And now that I have a full belly, I feel it."

"Curl up and get some sleep," he said. "I'll set a perimeter and then stay in the house while you rest."

"I seriously doubt I'll be able to nod off." There hadn't been a good night's sleep in weeks. She'd done little more than doze off long enough to refuel before a few more hours of work. Any noise, anything that went 'bump' was the equivalent of a shot of caffeine in her arm. Of course, being a new mom, she hadn't had a real night's sleep since the end of her second trimester of pregnancy.

"I'll be back," he said with a reassuring wink. "You're safe."

The thought of him leaving had her reaching for his hand to stop him. He did. Contact caused sensual shivers to skitter across her skin—skitters she did her best to ignore. An attraction wasn't just inconvenient, it was out of the question and wrong, no matter how much a little voice in the back of her head argued otherwise.

Did he feel the same electricity she did? The air practically sizzled with heat in between them. She chalked it up to missing being with the opposite sex even though she knew it couldn't be further from the truth. Dane was different, special. And she wanted to know more about him. It was the real reason she'd gone online to see what she could find out if she was being honest with herself.

"Don't go," she said, hating the shakiness in her voice. "It's been a really long time since I felt this safe." She figured he would chalk it up to her being on the run but the truth was that she hadn't felt truly safe in a very long time. Despite growing up with Lucas, she'd lost touch with who he was becoming in the past few years. And as long as she was being totally honest, the way she'd felt about him had changed too.

Lucas was everything familiar and reassuring. The fact

they'd known each other and had been a couple for most of her life comforted her. Most of their friends joked they were already married. She couldn't argue it felt that way most of the time. When he came home on leave, he wanted to stay home, pop a beer, and watch a game on TV.

Dane, on the other hand, threatened to shatter her carefully constructed walls.

Her stomach quivered when he stood this close, a sensation she'd never felt before, not even with Lucas. Her pulse raced and her heart thundered. The pull of attraction was earth to sun. He was like a blazing campfire in the freezing cold. And she didn't know what to do with the way he made her feel.

Dane's gaze locked onto someone or something out the window. He ducked down, breaking their connection. His muscles corded and his expression morphed. His gaze narrowed. His lips thinned. There was an absent quality to his eyes she'd seen one too many times.

"What is it?" she whispered.

"Someone's here," came the response.

7

"Get down on the floor." Dane stayed in a crouched position as he crab-walked to the window.

"Hello? It's me, if you're in there. Don't shoot," said a familiar voice.

"Eric?" Dane popped up to standing. His younger brother stood in the middle of the lawn, halfway between the cabin and the lake, waving his hands in the air. Dane turned his head to the side. "It's safe. You can sit up now, it's one of my brothers. Get back to work or take a nap. I'll handle this."

"Nap? Are you kidding me? I wouldn't miss the chance to meet your brother for the world," Catalina said with more amusement in her voice than he'd heard since he'd met her. There was fear too, and he was pretty sure an adrenaline rush caused that same voice to shake. "Besides, I'm thinking too hard about a problem with the code. Maybe if I relax or at the very least distract myself the answer will come to me."

"Suit yourself." Dane opened the door, trying to forget the sensations that had been coursing through his body a few minutes ago when Catalina had reached out to touch him. Besides, seeing his younger brother put a smile on Dane's face. He was also concerned and had a serious question. "How did you know where to find me?"

Eric, who was one of the bulkier Firebrands, could best be described as a tank. He had the Firebrand height, coming in at just shy of six feet five inches, and he was built like a linebacker. College recruiters had come knocking his junior year of high school but he'd turned them away, deciding to stay on and work the ranch for reasons Dane would never understand. Despite his brother's physical size and strength, he liked to work the back-office operations.

His brother broke into a run the minute he saw Dane, practically plowing him over and knocking him back a step as he met him on the porch.

"It's good to see you, man," Eric said, sounding like he had a frog in his throat. If Dane didn't know any better, he'd say his big tough brother was getting emotional. Eric patted Dane on the back before breaking free from the bear hug. The pat left Dane struggling for air.

"You too," Dane admitted. It was better than he realized. "You still didn't answer my question, though." If Eric found them, others might be able to.

"Jacob, but he made me promise not to tell anyone else. Said he didn't think you'd mind if I knew," Eric explained. "Don't take it out on him. I'm glad he let me know."

Dane had half a mind to give Jacob a call. This was precisely the reason he hadn't asked for permission to stay at the fishing cabin. He didn't want anyone to know he was staying there, including Jacob. Dane checked his anger because it was also really good to see his brother again. He didn't realize how much he missed Eric until now. Of all Dane's brothers, he'd been closest to Eric. The two of them had taken a lot of lip for being close to their twin cousins

Morgan and Nick. After they'd ganged up on Dane in middle school, he and Eric had worked out their differences.

There wasn't much Dane could do about Eric being here and a big part of him didn't want to anyway. The only thing left to do was invite him inside.

"Do you want to come in?" Dane surveyed the area, ensuring no one had followed his brother.

"I haven't seen you in..." Eric made a show of counting on his fingers. He cocked an eyebrow. "Five years?"

"Four and a half," he corrected. He'd done the math on the flight from Virginia.

"Yes, I want to come in and talk to my brother." Eric smiled and shook his head.

"Where did you park?" Dane needed to assess the potential damage.

"Nowhere around here. I'm on the other side of the lake," Eric supplied.

"Good." Dane put an arm around his brother as he passed by. "There's someone I'd like you to meet."

"Jacob didn't say you had company." Eric's eyebrows drew together.

"Because it's the other way around," Dane said.

"Now I really am confused," Eric said.

Dane opened the door, "I'm imposing on a friend."

His first instinct was to inform his brother of the situation. The more hands on deck, the better as far as he was concerned now that Eric was in the picture. But since this wasn't his story to tell, it was up to Catalina to make the call as to who was brought up to speed about her situation.

Eric took step inside and immediately removed his ballcap. He held it against his chest. "Ma'am."

"Catalina, this is my brother," Dane said.

She stood up and met Eric halfway from the couch to the door. "It's nice to meet you."

"Eric." He extended a hand, which she took. "Good to meet you, Catalina."

"My friend here is working on a complex computer programming problem," Dane explained.

"Wish I could offer some help. The best I can do with computers is work spreadsheets and e-mails," Eric said. Questions brewed behind his eyes, but he seemed to realize this wasn't the time to ask.

"I'm sure I'll figure it out," Catalina said, smiling. She had a much more relaxed posture than when the two of them had first met. "And I'd probably better get back to it."

"We'll just be over here." Dane motioned toward the table. "Or will the noise distract you?"

Catalina walked over to her backpack, reached in, and then pulled out a pair of noise-cancelling headphones. "That's what these are for. Believe it or not, I've done some of my best work at coffee shops. I like the hum of conversation and people moving around. It's probably weird but I find it comforting."

She excused herself before repositioning on the couch so that she'd have a full view of everything going on in the room. Her instincts were good. No one should sit with their back to the room unless they wanted a knife in it, although that rule shouldn't need to apply here. Dane was there to protect her and Eric would no sooner stab her in the back than drive a knife in his own chest. And yet he couldn't fault her for the move. He would have done the same thing.

Dane also wondered if part of the move was curiosity. She'd already gone online to search his name and learn more about his family. It was easy to find information. Of course, he would have preferred for her to ask him straight out rather than dig around where she would find untruths.

"How is home?" He joined his brother at the table.

"Different." Eric's eyebrow shot up. "Haven't you heard?"

"About the Marshall?" he asked. "It's the reason I came home."

"Well, yes, about the Marshall but there's been a whole dust storm kicked up since his passing." Eric gave Dane a look. "You really don't know?"

"I guess you'll have to fill me in." Dane shrugged his shoulders. He wasn't exactly on the family group message any longer and preferred it that way.

"Adam is married and has a kid." Eric's announcement nearly knocked Dane out of his chair. His jaw practically hit the floor.

"What? When did this happen?" His instinct was to go for his phone but, clearly, no one thought to shoot him a text. Or maybe they did. He'd changed numbers last year, a habit to keep him as off the grid as much as possible.

"Beginning of June," Eric stated.

"I'm no expert, but I'm pretty sure it takes a lot longer to cook a baby than a few weeks." Dane figured there was a bigger story there.

"Right. His on-again, off-again girlfriend Libby didn't tell him about the baby. There was something bad going down with her and her parents. I was out of town for most of it, to be honest, but the long and short of the story is that Prudence Owens wound up in possession of Angel, and then brought her to Adam. Apparently, she'd been taking a medication that mixed badly with something else and had short-term memory loss. They got it all sorted out and Adam found the love of his life in the process," Eric explained.

"What about Libby?" Dane asked.

Eric shook his head and frowned. "There was an investigation into her murder but she's gone."

Dane risked a glance at Catalina, who looked horrified by the news. As a new single mother, he could only imagine what might be going through her mind. "And the baby is okay?"

"A little girl. We call her Angel and she is." The way Eric beamed with pride about their niece touched Dane. Eric had always been a little rough around the edges. Seeing him soften while talking about Angel delivered a surprising blow to Dane in the chest.

"Can't wait to meet her then," he said. He didn't like babies for the most part and could never see himself with one, but he was happy for his brother. "And Adam's happy?"

"I've never seen him with a sappier smile or look more ridiculously content," Eric said. "Losing Libby has been hard on him. The two might have broken up a long time ago but losing her in that way...let's just say he cared a lot about what happened to the mother of his child."

"Sounds like I've missed a lot recently," Dane stated.

"You'll really be shocked when you hear about Brax," Eric said, his tone caused Dane's pulse to rise a couple of notches.

"What's going on with Brax?" Dane asked. "Are you going to tell me he's married with a kid?"

"Not with a kid but he is married," Eric said. "But that's not the big news."

Dane steadied himself for another bombshell.

"Turns out, our lovely father had an affair." Eric shot a look that said everything Dane needed to know about what was coming next. "Mom took Brax in as her own and never looked back. His birth mother died during childbirth, so his birth certificate was finagled to say he was Mom's child. He's actually thirty-six years old. They lied to make the numbers work."

"How did an entire town look the other way?" Dane asked. "A child shows up and no one asks questions?"

"You know how powerful the Marshall was." Eric had a point.

"I'm sure he couldn't have one of his grandchildren brought up outside of the ranch," Dane said low and under his breath. Dane had bolted after graduation in part to punish the man. He could admit that now even though he didn't see it clearly at the time. Eighteen, full of fight and testosterone, he'd needed an enemy he could see. But, right now, he cared more about how Brax had taken the news. Guilt that he wasn't here for his brother wrapped around him like a shroud. "What about Brax?"

He couldn't imagine how much this must have fractured Brax's relationship with their parents.

"About that." Eric paused for what seemed like a dramatic effect. "Do you remember Raleigh Perry?"

"How could I forget that little redheaded streak. She was mostly quiet but had a wild streak in her a mile wild," Dane said.

"Sorry for interrupting, but do you mean *the* Raleigh Perry?" Catalina asked from across the room. Her legs were crisscrossed and she had portable desk with the laptop on her lap, fingers on keyboard. Her jaw, however, nearly hit the piece of tech when it dropped open.

"Wait. What about Raleigh? I'm guessing her music is doing okay if Catalina knows her," Dane said.

"Know her? Are you kidding me?" Catalina's fingers danced across the keyboard. A song filled the room. "*The Loft* is probably the best song ever written."

It was good. There was no denying.

"Hold on a second," Dane said. "As memory serves, I always found her in *our* loft."

Eric nodded. "Turns out, that's where her career started. She was up there learning to write songs."

He listened for a long moment.

"She's good," he admitted, a burst of pride filled his chest for the kid. "She sure doesn't sound fifteen anymore."

"No, she doesn't. And you know Mom. She's practically bursting with pride for Raleigh's success since she was like a second Mom to her," Eric said.

"I read something in the news about a bomb threat," Catalina said as her fingers danced across the keyboard.

Dane's gaze flew to Eric.

"It's true. She came back to Lone Star Pass to wait it out while the feds investigated and found love with—"

"No," Dane interrupted. "You gotta be kidding me."

"Raleigh and Brax tied the knot and he's about to join her on tour," Eric supplied.

"Well, I'll be..."

Life hadn't stayed the same in his old hometown after all.

"I'm guessing Brax and Mom are on good terms." Dane hoped.

"She had a hard time with revealing the truth to Brax," Eric said.

"I can imagine," Catalina said. She shook her head. "Sorry. This is none of my business. Forget I'm here."

Click. Clack. Clack.

Her gaze dropped to the screen and her fingers flew across the keyboard.

"A lot has happened since the Marshall passed away."

Dane issued a sharp sigh, processing the changes in his family.

"Brax and Dad aren't really talking, and neither is Corbin, but he has his reasons," Eric said.

"We all do," Dane agreed.

"There's more but this is out there even for our family." Eric adjusted his watch.

"Give it to me straight then." Dane was already in shock. Might as well take the full shot now. Get it all over with so he could start processing this new reality.

"Kellan is divorced," Eric said.

"I didn't even realize he'd gotten married." This was news to Dane. But then that's what he got for staying away for the past four years.

"Liv Holden." Eric shot a warning look. "The whole situation was a mess and ended up with Uncle Keif in jail."

"Hold on a second." Dane put his hand up like he could somehow physically stop his brother from continuing. "Corbin's best friend Liv?"

"The very one," Eric stated.

"What was she doing marrying Kellan?" Dane had always believed Corbin and Liv should be together despite his brother's long-term relationship with another woman—a relationship that never should have lasted as long as it did.

"Her mom was in an accident," Eric said on a sigh. "It was rough. She was a mess. Corbin got engaged. Kellan swooped in."

"You've got to be kidding me." Everyone with eyes could see that Corbin and Liv should have ended up together as a couple. There wasn't a reality in which that shouldn't have happened. "I'm guessing she figured out Kellan was a jerk."

"Things got heated. He was supposedly sending threatening texts. Turned out her cousin Jody was involved. Kellan swears he never sent the messages. I believe that much from him. Uncle Keif was trying to force her to leave town and give up her family home."

"What a jerk." Dane couldn't believe what he'd missed. Four and a half years ago, literally nothing had changed. Now, overnight, the family had grown exponentially and absurd didn't seem like nearly big enough a word to cover events in recent weeks.

"You got that right." Eric fidgeted with his watch again.

"Is Uncle Keif out of jail now?" Dane asked, figuring a few strings would have been pulled to make that happen, if he was guilty and was still awaiting trial.

"He's been cleared of wrongdoing but Ed Roberts, the older Realtor gentleman, was murdered by Jody. Uncle Keif promised the house to him if he could get rid of Liv," Eric continued. "But he never intended things to go so far. He turned himself in the minute Ed was murdered."

"Sounds like the town's been through a lot lately." Dane would need a minute to process all this news. "And the family. Both sides."

Eric nodded.

"How is Mom?" Dane fisted his hands, flexing and releasing his fingers a few times trying to work off the tension. His biggest regret was not staying in better contact with his mother. He assumed she had her hands full, but she was one of the kindest people he'd ever met and didn't deserve any of this. All the more reason to hate his father for forcing Dane to lie to her about what happened all those years ago.

A secret he would take to his grave.

8

Catalina listened to the conversation between Dane and his brother. She couldn't help but overhear, which didn't excuse the fact she also actively listened. Her heart went out to his family, but she heard something in his voice when his father was mentioned—something that made her want to dig deeper and understand why he seemed to hate the man. The mention of his uncle wasn't much better, but his reaction to his father caught her attention. Had something happened between the two of them to drive a wedge?

It was probably exhaustion that had her wanting to hear more about his family and block out the code that wasn't working. She stared at the picture of her son. He'd brought a whole new level of meaning to the word *family* when he came into the world. She'd never been one to believe a child completed a woman any more than a man did. The best relationships, she was learning the hard way, seemed to come from two whole people. People who lift each other up, not tear them down. The last few years of her relationship with Lucas had deteriorated. When he was home, he wanted to check her phone to see if she was talking to guys. The accusations came out of seemingly nowhere. The stress of the job seemed to weigh on him more and more.

Not being able to save him frustrated her to no end. Still did.

Could she finish this app, get it in the right hands, and make certain no soldier ever suffered the same fate? It was so unfair Luke would never know his father. *He would,* a little voice in the back of her mind countered. She would make certain he knew of his father's bravery, his big heart, and his ridiculous sense of humor.

Filled with a new resolve, Catalina took in a deep breath and focused. An hour later, she'd made progress. It wasn't much and she wouldn't classify it as great. But she'd take what she could get. If football games could be won by inches, she'd creep her way across this finish line. Once she had a workable program, she needed to reach out to Hansen. There was no point making contact before she had a finished product.

The money she earned from the sale would set her and Luke up for a few years, give her time to regroup and find a job. But, most importantly, it would give her time to bond with her son. It would be easy to give in to the tidal wave of emotion threatening to suck her under due to being separated from her baby right now. It took everything she had inside her to set those feelings aside. Focus would reunite her with Luke.

Besides, his safety was everything to her.

The temptation to call and check on him practically burned a hole in her chest. The rules she'd set had to be followed. No contact. A moment of weakness could reveal his location. No way could she risk it.

Dane stood up a second after his brother. The two embraced in a hug that warmed Catalina's heart. Her parents divorced when she was in kindergarten. Her father remarried and started a new life, apparently forgetting his old one because she never heard from him. Not birthdays. Not holidays. Not when there was a full moon. Not when there wasn't a full moon. He'd basically dropped out of existence.

Her mother did her 'parenting time' as she'd called it. Once Catalina graduated high school, her mother moved to Florida and the last picture of her on her social media page was of her on a yacht with a group of overly tanned people from a singles group she'd apparently joined. Faye reclaimed her maiden name, Dodd.

A surprising tear rolled down Catalina's cheek thinking about her family. Her grandmother was the only constant in her life. If she was honest with herself, her mother had checked out years before the move.

Catalina needed to take a catnap. The only time her emotions got to her was when she was tired.

Dane walked Eric outside as she closed her laptop and set it on the coffee table. She curled up on her side and closed her eyes. By the time she opened them again, it was dark outside.

She bolted upright and glanced around, trying to break through the sleep fog and get her bearings.

"You're okay," the soothing masculine voice came from across the room. It slid over her and through her, waking up places she didn't know existed until meeting Dane.

"How long did I sleep?" A blanket slid off her and onto the floor. She reached down to pick it up, realizing he must've placed it over her while she slept.

"It's almost ten o'clock," he said.

"At night?" She'd lost the whole day. The kitchen light flipped on, bathing her in light.

"Are you hungry?" he asked.

"Yes," she said, needing a cold shower to shake her out of the half-asleep fog. "But I'd like to wake up first."

"There's coffee or more Coke if you'd rather have one," he said.

"I grabbed the last one this morning. Did you leave?" Panic tried to close her throat up and make it impossible to breathe.

"I said I would stay with you." There was a twinge of hurt in his voice. He seemed more than a little wounded she would doubt his word.

"Right. Your brother was here. He must've gone for supplies," she said. "Sorry."

"No need to apologize." There was a vacancy to his voice now that she hadn't picked up on before. Did it have to do with talking about his family? The blankness in his eyes threw her for another loop.

"Is everything okay?" She rubbed her blurry eyes, adding caffeine to her list of wants.

"Peachy." His one-word response sent up another alarm, which triggered a memory.

Lucas had done the same when he came home. She'd given him space and the emotional distance grew as he seemed to sink deeper and deeper into a pit she had no power to pull him out of.

"For all intents and purposes, I'm putting my life in your hands." She cleared her throat. Finding the right words wasn't easy and she was so far out of her comfort zone right now.

"Agreed."

"I hope you'll forgive me for being so forward but I want

to help." She barely got those words out before Dane was up pacing in the kitchen.

"And I'm suddenly your pet project?" he shot back.

"No. But we are going to be spending time together—"

"So I can help *you*." He raked a hand through his hair. "Let's keep that part straight if you don't mind."

"I was just trying—"

"To what?" he cut her off. "Armchair shrink me?"

"No."

"Good," he said. "Because you need to get one thing straight. I don't need your help."

Those words spoken with so much fire made her want to curl up in a ball. She wasn't sure why she cared so much about Dane, except that she did. From somewhere deep inside, she was already attached to this man. She needed to know he was going to be all right when this was all said and done.

After a few breaths meant to calm her nerves, she stood up. She wrung her hands together, unsure of what she was going to say or do once she got to him. Rather than debate her next actions, she just rolled with what felt natural.

The room was small, so she essentially blocked his exit. He stopped dead center of the room and practically glared at her. There was so much intensity in his stare...and pain. There was no way she could walk away without at least trying no matter how hard he pushed her away. She would never be able to forgive herself if she did it again.

Another deep breath, and she placed her hands on his chest and locked gazes with him.

"If I'm putting my trust in you, then you could at least do me the courtesy of being honest with me, but if you're not okay and are off your game, I need to know. Because it could affect me and I have a child to make it home to."

"Believe me when I say none of this will impact your safety. You have my word on that point," he promised as he clenched his back teeth.

"I don't know what happened in your past, Dane. You certainly don't have to tell me. I'm just sorry for whatever you've had to endure because I see a strong person here." She had no idea where the words were coming from. She was speaking from the heart, hoping some of her words resonated. "And I think you're amazing."

Dane clenched his back teeth again, and a storm brewed behind those pure blue eyes. He gripped her hands at the wrists and issued a sharp sigh.

When he didn't respond verbally, she pushed up to her tiptoes and pressed a kiss to his lips. Then, she turned and walked away.

Dane stood there for a long moment, vacillating between anger and shock. The words struck a chord. The kiss had been tender. And then anger flooded him again. He didn't need to be fixed. Besides, it was too late. He couldn't break down those walls if he wanted to. They were too embedded. Pain was all he knew, especially when it came to his father. Thinking about Brodie Firebrand caused Dane's hands to fist and anger to roar through him.

Being forced to keep his father's secret had messed with a young boy's mind. Remembering caused all kinds of pent-up frustration to flood him.

The water turned on in the other room, breaking into the heavy moment. He shoved those thoughts down deep, where they belonged, forcing himself not to replace them with thoughts of Catalina naked in the shower.

Dane dropped to the floor and fired off fifty pushups. He needed to work off some of his frustration or risk losing his temper, which wasn't something he would allow himself to do with Catalina. Her words struck him in a dark place—a place he didn't want or need to shed light on. Anger ripped through him like a spring tornado. He refused to let the rage win. Sit-ups were next, followed by burpees. He'd do anything at this point to work off the excess energy. Being inside all day hadn't been good for him.

As soon as he heard the water shut off in the next room, he finished his workout and shouldered his rucksack. The minute Catalina stepped into the living room, he made a beeline for the bathroom, gripping the strap of his rucksack so tight his knuckles turned white.

Her voice kept creeping into his thoughts during the workout. Her strong but somehow delicate tone embedding itself in his mind. She was special. There was no doubt about it. And based on their conversation earlier, he doubted Lucas told her nearly enough. The man might have spoken highly of her when he was around other guys, but did he ever tell her how beautiful and intelligent she was?

Because the sadness behind her eyes said she hadn't been loved anywhere close to the way she deserved. And it wasn't Dane's mistake to correct no matter how easy it would have been to dip his head down and claim those pink lips of hers.

"Help yourself. There are readymade dinners in the fridge," he practically grunted as he walked past her.

Being in the same house with her without touching her was going to be more difficult than it should be.

"Okay," she said, her voice trailing over him.

Shower. Cold. Now.

As much as Dane tried, he couldn't run enough cold

water to cool his hot temper. Normally, he didn't have a problem with containment. So, he'd have to watch himself around her.

By the time he exited the shower and dried off, he'd managed to think about at least one other thing besides Catalina. The way his brother wanted to step up and help had reminded him of the good parts of being a Firebrand. It had been a little too easy to block those out while overseas. The memory of his father and grandfather's actions had choked out all that was good.

Dane needed to fix it. When this was over, he planned to go see his mother. Maybe even stay at his home on the ranch. Or, just to stick it the Marshall who never liked anyone in his house, maybe he'd stay at the main house instead.

The thought made him smirk. Sounds like he just figured out his next step when he secured Catalina.

By the time he entered the main living rooms, the smell of his mother's homemade meatballs hit him square in the face. He might have suppressed a whole lot of things about being brought up a Firebrand, but his Italian mother's meatballs weren't one of them.

"These are amazing," Catalina said, lifting one off her plate with her fork. "You should try them."

"They're an old family recipe," he said, managing a much calmer and more collected voice now. "And they smell just like the last time I tasted them four and a half years ago."

"You haven't been home in over four years?" Her mouth fell open.

"When you're over there it just gets easier and easier to stay there." The admission surprised him.

"Lucas came home less and less over the years." She

pushed the meatball around with her fork. "I never asked why. I just thought he was working through things and life would somehow get back to normal once he got out."

Was that the reason she'd pushed him to talk earlier? Dane heated a plate of spaghetti and meatballs, listening to what Catalina had to say.

"He slipped away from me," she said softly.

His unspoken question was answered with her statement.

She didn't look up at him and he suspected she was trying to hide tears. Catalina, he was beginning to realize, was one of the bravest people he would ever meet. She was taking on her boss, putting her own life at risk to stop her program from getting into the wrong hands, and she single-handedly went into hiding while finishing coding. All of this after giving birth and finding a place to hide her son.

"I don't think you hear this nearly enough." He took his plate out of the microwave and joined her at the table where she'd set out two places. "But you're also an amazing person, Catalina. Lucas was lucky to have you."

"Thank you," she said, not looking directly at him. Her appreciation for the compliment came through in her voice. "At least now I have you here and I'm rested. Dinner was the best meal I've had in...I can't remember how long. All I need now is caffeine and I can get back to cracking at the code."

Dane's cell buzzed, and the alarm sounded. He must have made a face because Catalina dropped her fork.

"What is it?" she asked. "What's wrong?"

"Someone is coming. We have to go."

9

"How much time do we have?" Catalina hopped up and was on her feet in two seconds. She picked up her plate and started toward the sink.

"Leave the dishes," Dane said, already moving toward his military-issue bag. "We have to go *now*."

The careful emphasis he placed on the last word caused her heart to drop. She set the plate back down on the table and rushed toward her backpack. The laptop went in first followed by the lap desk. She scrambled into the next room and joined Dane who was already gathering up her toiletries and clothes, tossing them inside her suitcase.

Less than three minutes later, they were crouched down low and moving toward the door.

"Key," he said, holding out his flat palm.

She reached inside the side pocket of her backpack, located it, and then handed it over.

"Eric will move your rental." He tossed the key toward the sedan, linked their fingers, and then headed toward the tree line in the opposite direction.

Normally, Catalina wouldn't hand over keys to a rental

car to a near stranger, except it felt like she'd known Dane for years already. She tried to chalk it up to him being familiar because he'd served in the same unit as Lucas, but it wasn't true. Lightning had struck the minute she'd seen Dane, and she'd known he was going to be an important person in her life. Could he be in Luke's as well?

Branches slapped at her face as Dane pushed the pace through the trees. He seemed to know exactly where he was headed, while she couldn't be more lost. Her lungs burned, her stomach cramped, and her thighs screamed, but he kept pushing. It took a minute for her eyes to adjust to the dark. There was no light out here.

When she slowed and he practically dragged her, he urged her to keep moving. She refused to be the one to slow them down. All she had to carry was a backpack. He'd taken the suitcase along with his own bag, and still managed to hold her hand.

His eyesight must be near perfect, and adaptable because hers was just beginning to adjust to the darkness surrounding them. All she could hear clearly was the snap of twigs underneath their shoes and the slap of branches.

Dane finally stopped and tugged her down until she crouched low. He seemed to have barely broken a sweat meanwhile, she sounded like a steam engine roaring down a track. She squeezed her side, trying to abate the cramp. No use.

Questions surfaced. Where were they? Who was coming? How long were they going to stay in the woods? Would they be able to return to the cabin? Did she forget anything that could identify her? Instinct told her to keep quiet.

She'd been so close to fixing another bug in the program before crashing on the couch. An answer came to her while in the shower a little while ago. Her fingers itched to get back to coding. The caffeine boost was no longer needed. Adrenaline had done the trick. Blood pulsed through her veins and her heart thumped inside her ribcage.

"We're spending the night out here," he finally said. His voice was low and gravelly. "How much battery do you have?"

"Enough to code for five hours and thirty-five minutes," she stated. "I should have been plugged in this whole time. Then, I would have more."

"I have an auxiliary charger. Let's hope that gets you through until morning," he said. "We'll have a new plan by then."

"Hold on a minute. We can't sleep out here...can we?" she asked, panic building. The most outdoorsy she'd ever been was the occasional picnic or outdoor concert. Even then mosquitoes seemed to consider her a favorite meal.

"Do you have a better idea?" His voice was a study in calm.

Right. He was used to living in much worse conditions. It was hot. She was sticky. Complaining would do no good. Plus, it wouldn't change the situation. Issuing a sharp sigh, she said, "No."

Her brain picked that moment to remind her she hadn't thanked him for everything he was already doing for her. This didn't seem like the right time to bring it up, so she set the thought aside with a promise to tell him later.

"When I say we'll stay out here, I didn't mean in this exact spot," his tone softened when he must have heard the panic in hers. "Follow me."

This didn't seem like the right time to point out the obvious fact she didn't have much of a choice. Unless she wanted to be stranded in the woods and eaten by mosquitoes or whatever else was out there and decided that she'd taste good.

But, hey, she refused to complain. She could do this and much more. *Chin up, shoulders back* was pretty much her life mantra. It had gotten her through Lucas's funeral, through a pregnancy on her own, and through childbirth. Being the snack of a mosquito wasn't going to take her down. Period.

After walking until it felt like her feet might fall off, she saw a structure in the trees. Her heart galloped. "Are we...?"

She couldn't bring herself to finish the question while she was unsure if she could handle the disappointment if the answer was no. A treehouse? Aside from taking her back to good memories in her childhood, it had four walls and a floor. There'd be no sleeping on the ground because, last she checked, there were all kinds of hazards there. Fire ants to name one. Getting bit by one of those stung like crazy. She'd already thought of mosquitoes but those could fly. But, hey, beggars couldn't be choosers.

Plus, being in the trees would put them in the breeze.

"How do you know about this place?" Catalina asked. Her eyes had adjusted to the dark a while ago. She should have kept track of how long they'd been walking and from which direction instead of placing her complete trust in Dane.

But it was Dane Firebrand. If she couldn't trust him, she might as well cash in her chips. He was one of the most honorable people she'd ever met and the few times Lucas had mentioned him, he had nothing but respect for the man. He'd said things like, "*He's quiet but I never question whether or not he has my back.*"

Whoever Lucas had complete faith in was good enough for Catalina. Of course, her instincts said she could trust him too. There was something special about the man.

"I grew up around here. Remember? Hang on. I'll be right back." He surveyed the area before climbing the wood posts that had been screwed into the tree. Thankfully, the treehouse wasn't too high in the air in the event they need to make a quick exit. Being up there would give them a height advantage too. Dane could keep an eye out while she coded.

Dane climbed back down, a little lighter this time. His backpack was missing. When he climbed up the second time, he took her suitcase with him. His third trip, he insisted on being the one to carry her backpack up.

"After you," he said after surveying the area again, a constant reminder of the danger they were in.

Catalina climbed up and scooted across the flooring. A piece of scrap carpet had been placed on top of the wood planks. It was surprisingly comfortable. The treehouse was one room with windows that allowed the breeze to come through. Other than that, the place was sparse. There was a small chest on one side and that was it as far as furniture went. Not surprising.

"The carpet is nice," she said. She wouldn't be able to stand upright in the treehouse. Sitting was comfortable enough to get through a few hours.

"Someone is keeping the place up. I imagine local kids still come here. It's summer and they'll be out of school, so this will only be good for tonight."

Under different circumstances, spending the whole night in a treehouse with Dane would cause her pulse to rise. As of now, she couldn't afford the distraction.

DANE REACHED for the small chest. He opened it and found a couple of sticks that had one end whittled down to form a sharp point, and, therefore, a weapon. *Nice.* There was a small Swiss Army knife that looked like it had been left out in the rain for a month, the blades rusty. It might come in handy. He pulled a few twenties out of his wallet and dropped them in the chest before returning it to its original position.

Glancing over at Catalina, he noticed she was shifting side-to-side on her bottom, no doubt trying to get comfortable. Even under these circumstances, her creamy skin glowed. Shadows played across her face, highlighting those cornflower blue eyes. There wasn't a man alive who wouldn't be attracted to her beauty, or so he tried to tell himself. Was he trying to ease the guilt of his attraction?

The short answer was *yes*. When she'd stood toe-to-toe with him in the kitchen earlier, he'd nearly lost his tightly gripped control. Dane shoved the thought aside. The situation had been avoided. No damage had been done. Because all he'd wanted to do in that moment was haul her against his chest and claim those pink lips of hers.

Granted, she'd kissed him. It had been nothing more than a peck. Again, nothing had happened that couldn't be recovered from. The last thing Dane wanted Catalina to feel after spending time with him was regret.

So, he bagged his attraction toward her and moved on. Too bad her spring rain and flowery scent filled his senses in the cramped space, reminding him how good she smelled and how much his fingers longed to touch her creamy skin.

Great job bagging the attraction, Firebrand.

He watched as she tried to prop herself up against the wall and wrangle her laptop out of its special pocket in her backpack. She got set up and then straightened her back. She slumped forward and then straightened up again, clearly struggling to get comfortable.

Dane grabbed his rucksack and crawled over, placing it behind her back. This close, her spring flower scent filled his senses, making rational thought next to impossible. The air between them charged with electrical current that he could tell she felt based on the look of hunger in her eyes—hunger he couldn't afford to see. Hunger that had him reaching a hand up to run his fingers along her jawline, and then down her neck.

She swallowed like her throat had suddenly dried up.

"Dane." The sound of his name rolling off her tongue corded his already taut muscles.

"Yeah?" was all he could manage to say in response. His attempt at coming off as causal fell flat.

"Can I ask you a favor?" Her voice slid over him and through him, clouding his already foggy judgment.

He couldn't remember the last time a woman's voice had this effect on him.

"Go ahead." Their faces were mere inches apart. Too close for Dane to be able to think clearly. He searched her gaze for a sign he should back away. Saw none. In fact, the more he looked into her eyes, the more he saw the signal to go ahead. But to do what?

"Kiss me," she said, her words breathed out softly, answering the question on his mind.

Dane refused to overthink this. Her request was simple. A kiss. She was in a life and death situation and her biology was telling her to grab hold of the closest person and affirm life.

There wasn't more to it than that. Whatever chemistry was happening between them wasn't special, he tried to convince himself. And it worked. Right up until he closed the distance between them and pressed his lips to hers.

Her hands came up to his shoulders. Her fingernails dug

into his skin through his t-shirt. Her lips moved against his, inviting him to take more.

She moaned against his mouth, parted her lips, and teased his tongue inside. She tasted like peppermint. Dane deepened the kiss, bringing his hand up to cup her face to position her for better access.

The next thing he knew, she'd shoved him backward until he sat on his backside. Her laptop was off her lap and she'd climbed onto his. There was so much fire and sizzle, and hunger in their kisses, Dane could see himself losing control with her.

A fleeting thought he needed to rein in what was happening between them was quickly dismissed. Denim was the only barrier between him and the apex of her thighs.

Dane tugged at her bottom lip, and she bit down on his. Every tongue stroke was matched until they were both gasping for air. Need was a physical force. She brought her hands up, tunneling her fingers in his hair as their tongues teased, teeth nipped until all he could think was...*more.*

He dropped his hands to her thighs, gripping them and squeezing as she rocked against him. He'd never felt so much need spring up so quickly in his entire life.

And then he opened his eyes. She opened hers. An unspoken moment happened between them—a moment that said another time, another place, and there'd be no stopping their sexual attraction. The current running from her and through him was the strongest he'd ever experienced. What was it about forbidden fruit that made it taste so much better? And this was most definitely off limits. Time was a luxury they didn't have, so he issued a sharp sigh and did his level best to collect himself.

Catalina tucked her hair behind her ears and leaned

back, creating enough distance in between them for Dane to regain more control. For a few minutes there, he'd just gone with what he was feeling. It was foreign to him to allow instinct to take over. The sex he'd had in the past was incredible, but he realized making love to Catalina would be in a whole new stratosphere. He'd never taken someone to bed that he wouldn't be able to get out of his mind.

He'd just broken one of his cardinal rules.

"This should help with bugs." Dane grabbed a couple of bug repellent wipe packets out of the side pocket of his bag. He handed one to Catalina before reclaiming his seat on the opposite side of the treehouse, balancing out the weight.

"I should have known you'd be prepared for anything," she said before adding, "thank you."

"It's a good idea to keep your monitor brightness as low as possible," he said with a nod. He was preaching to the choir with his remark but hopefully she realized he was trying to be helpful. He checked his cell phone. "I don't have any bars out here. Doesn't surprise me, just thought you should be aware."

"I can't even create a hotspot since there's no service out here. Plus, I doubt this disposable phone is capable anyway." She slicked her tongue across her bottom lip, and he forced himself to look away. Those few moments when they'd given need the reins had put them at their most vulnerable. As much as he believed it was safe up here in the treehouse, he couldn't afford to let his guard down like that again. And neither could she.

10

Catalina stretched her arms out and rolled her head around a couple of times, trying to release some of the tension in her neck. Her battery was getting low and she'd solved one of the bugs in the programming. Progress was slow but she was making some at least.

She leaned her head against the wall and closed her eyes. Big mistake. Her thoughts drifted back to the scorching hot kiss. Every time.

"I have power bars if you're hungry," Dane's voice had a habit of moving over her and through her, stirring places she didn't need to think about while on a deadline and trying to stay one step ahead of jerks who wanted to erase her.

"I'll take you up on that," she said, yawning. She wasn't tired so much as tired of sitting in one place. Her bottom hurt and so did her lower back. Dane's bag helped but couldn't possibly save her back.

Dane came over to her side of the space, and then reached beside her and into his bag. His presence right in front of her caused too many competing sensations to flood her. He handed over a bar, palmed one for himself, and then retreated. There was something else in his hand.

"What's that?" She opened the bar and polished it off in a matter of seconds. It was almost pure protein, tasted like eating peanut butter from a jar, and was surprisingly filling.

"This chocolate square is the equivalent of drinking a cup of coffee." He held one in between his thumb and fore-fingers.

"Are you serious? Because I'd kill for both right now." She heard the word roll off her tongue casually and caught herself. Strange how that and other words were taking on a new meaning now that she was on the run and fighting for her own life. Kal Sutton would be willing to protect his secret in any and every way. He would silence her in a heart-beat. The thought made a shiver race down her spine.

Dane tossed a chocolate square to her. She missed, but it landed on her thigh. She snapped it up, opened it and savored the flavor. It tasted like a mocha, her favorite indul-gence. "This chocolate square is amazing."

"Agreed," Dane said, his voice raw and husky. Sexy.

"In the first few weeks after Luke was born, I needed a reason to get out of the house and interact with people who weren't one hundred percent dependent on me to live," she said. "There's this little coffee shop down the street from my house that I visited on a daily basis. The baristas got to know me so well, they started making my order the minute I walked through the door. This reminds me of my mochas." She held up the wrapper, and then scooted the lap desk off her legs before crisscrossing them.

"I can't imagine how intense it must have been to bring a kid into the world on your own. I doubt I could do it." Dane's admission caught her off guard.

"You'd be surprised what you can do when life throws a

curveball your way," she said. And then for reasons she couldn't explain added, "Lucas and my relationship had been over for years when he disappeared. We just didn't know it yet or were too stubborn to quit."

Dane's eyebrow shot up. Questions danced behind his eyes. To his credit, he didn't ask.

"We'd been together since we were kids." She shrugged. "I loved him deeply, so I hope you won't take this the wrong way. I hadn't been in love with him for the past five years, maybe longer."

"Then, why string him along?" He seemed to hear how that sounded when he cocked his head to one side. "Why keep the relationship going? Seems like it would just be leading him on."

"I planned to marry him," she defended. "There was no way I was going to back out of the promise we made to each other. The promise I made to him." She issued a sharp sigh. "He changed. Being overseas changed him. And I didn't know how to ever get him back. But that didn't mean I would give up on us."

"Ever think it was *his* job to keep his mental game strong and not yours?" There was no judgment in his tone. He asked the question like he was reading a spreadsheet for her old department's budget.

"Under any other circumstances, I probably would. I just felt like these were extenuating. He went into the military because he couldn't afford to go to college and he wanted to provide a future for us," she said. "We were eighteen. What did we know?"

"Young people make mistakes. I can't imagine planning out my entire future at eighteen years old," he agreed.

"And yet you decided to stay with the military for your career," she said.

"Years later. It happened by default. My tour would end, and I would re-sign. I went into it thinking I'd do a few years and then get out." He ripped open the chocolate package before tossing the square in his mouth and chewing on it. "I kept thinking I'd leave when I had a better idea. None ever came and I was good at being a soldier."

"The best, according to Lucas," she admitted.

Dane shook his head. "There's always someone out there who will eventually be better than you."

He held up his right hand and she could see a tremor.

"Nerve damage," he said.

"How did it happen?" she asked.

"Got too close to a blast and came home with a present. Nerve damage," he stated.

"Medically boarded?" She'd already guessed, so he would only be confirming what she already knew. Still, it seemed important for him to talk about it.

"That's right. Now, I'm out and shy of my twenty years," he said.

"You don't need the money." She put her hands up in the surrender position, palms out. "I know you already said you want to make your own way."

"It's true," he said. "I also wanted to stick it to my grandfather, and my father if I'm honest. Show them both I didn't need their money."

"Sounds rebellious." She smiled but picked up on the current of anger in his voice at the mention of his father and grandfather.

"That's me," he teased, rewarding her with a smile that melted the few defenses she'd constructed since the bone-melting kiss.

"Can I ask what you have against your family? You seem really close with your brother and he dropped everything to help us." She wandered into dangerous territory based on the way his smile faded and his gaze narrowed.

"My brother isn't the problem." There was a finality to his tone that said he was done talking about it.

Taking a slow breath, Catalina continued, "You came home to pay your respects. Why?"

"That conversation is classified and you don't have the clearance," his tone dropped a few octaves, a low rumble.

"He must have meant something to you," she pressed on.

"I already missed one funeral for someone I cared about. I had no plans to miss another even if I didn't have the same feeling." He put his hand up to stop her from asking another question. "This subject is closed."

"Saying goodbye is hard. Believe me. I know firsthand," she said.

"At least you loved the person who died." Dane seemed to hear those words as they came out of his mouth.

She brought her hand up to cover hers as she looked away. He might not have meant for his comment to come across as cruel, but it had scored a direct hit. She might have loved Lucas in her own way, but her feelings toward him never made her stomach quiver or her breath catch with just one look.

And she almost said those words out loud. She also realized Dane had finally opened up and talked to her about something important. He'd shut down but this was progress —progress she'd take.

DANE PULLED his legs up toward his chest, resting his elbows on his knees. Talking wasn't something he was normally great at or enjoyed doing. Between the long conversation with Eric and speaking to Catalina, he figured he'd spoken as many words in the past twenty-four hours as he had in the past year in total.

Talking to Catalina was odd because he actually liked it. He could talk to her all night and never get bored or tired. The subject of his grandfather was off limits. So was the subject of his relationship with his father. Period.

He needed to redirect the conversation.

"Are you telling me you would have married Lucas, and then lived happily ever after? Stayed with him for the rest of your life?" He turned the tables and she sucked in a burst of air. Had he crossed a line? He half expected her to refuse to answer.

Instead, she took in a slow breath and said, "Lucas never would have abandoned me if something happened that changed me. I can't answer your question as to whether or not I'd be happy if Lucas and I had been able to get married. Our connection was deep. But I know I never would have been happy if I'd walked away because he came home broken."

Her devotion struck Dane harder than a hammer to the ribs. And he knew exactly what that particular brand of pain felt like. The butt of a gun to his head. A shot that grazes his arm. Those, among other things. Things that sometimes changed a person. He'd seen it happen with his team and had sworn not to let it affect him in the same way.

But then, he never let anyone get close enough to him to notice if he came home different. Besides, it would be impossible to tell from arm's length, which is where he kept most people. And the fact he'd missed the signs with Lucas was another gut punch.

There was a pull toward Catalina he couldn't ignore if he tried. Dane found himself in strange territory because he didn't *want* to try to push her away. Still, there were a couple of topics that remained off limits and some secrets left buried.

"Any chance it's safe to take a walk?" She interrupted his thoughts.

He moved around the room, checking in between cracks in the wood. The sun was high in the sky. The breeze was gone. The temperature inside the treehouse was rising.

Catalina fanned herself with a notebook from her backpack. Her cheeks flushed and it made her even more beautiful if that was possible. He doubted it was. Physically, she had all the features a person would consider perfect. High cheekbones. Perfectly symmetrical features. A true beauty. Those features were icing on the cake. She was smart. Loyal. Kind. And her compassion shone through those cornflower blue eyes of her. So did her stubbornness.

There was so much more to her than attractive physical features. She had a depth few people would ever know. He'd heard people like her referred to as old souls. They understood pain and suffering. They understood people. And they had empathy beyond comparison.

They were rare. She was rare. And under different circumstances, he could see himself with someone like her in the long haul. But she needed another soldier in her life like he needed a bullet through his skull.

After he'd checked the perimeter, he checked the exit. Dane listened. It was surprising to him how many of his enemies gave themselves away because they lacked the ability to be quiet. Sand didn't make a whole lot of noise but he'd encountered enemies who breathed too heavily. Or whispered while out on patrol. Death wish?

It was possible. People got comfortable. Let their guards down.

If he was going to let his carefully constructed walls down with anyone, it would be someone like Catalina.

"It's clear. Just in case, we'll leave our belongings here. We can take a walk through the trees, possibly find cell reception. There was a place over by the lake but we'd have to hike back toward the cabins and there's a chance the kids who left behind the chest will come back." He got to be the best by taking everything into consideration. "On second thought, it's probably safer to stash these in my vehicle."

"You think it's okay to go back there?" Panic widened her eyes.

"We'll know when I get cell coverage. Eric planned to stick around and keep his eyes on the vehicle," he said.

"Did he have a description?" she asked.

"An SUV with blacked out windows and temporary plates is all he said. I didn't wait around to find out if he got a description of the driver and possible passengers." Dane figured Eric would have reached out to him by now. There would be no reason for the SUV to stick around considering there was no trace of Catalina at the cabin. For a split second, he thought about Jacob's parents. Were they in danger? No. Eric would never allow the SUV to do anything to the older couple. Besides, the driver would want to stay under the radar. Even if he saw Jacob's parents, he wouldn't risk hurting them. If he was really good, they would never know he was around.

"That gives me the chills just thinking about someone like that looking for me." She shook like she was trying to shake it off. "This whole thing is new to me. It's awful."

"You get used to it," he said.

"Do you?" Her eyebrow shot up like she really wanted the answer.

"When you know what you're fighting for, it gets easier."

He climbed down and ensure the area was clear before motioning for her to toss down the bags. He caught them and set them to the side before helping her down. "Our team did a lot of strategic rescue work, which generally meant we were the guys you sent in when a consulate had to be evacuated. When innocent lives were at stake, your focus becomes clear."

"Much like what you're doing for me right now," she said so low he almost didn't hear her.

"Yes, to a point," he said. "I never knew the people I helped before. This is different. I know you."

The look she gave him next told him she felt the same way. "Most people would think I'm crazy for saying this, considering we've only been around each other for a matter of hours, but the minute I saw you, it was like I'd known you my entire life."

He nodded, not wanting to put too much stock into the comment. It was true for him though. Dangerous, but true.

"I haven't really thanked you for everything you're doing for me. I'm guessing it has a whole lot to do with your friendship with Lucas and less to do with me personally. I appreciate it anyway. Because of you, I have a hope that I'll actually go home to my son in a few days." She reached over and clasped their hands together. Her hand was small in comparison to his. Hers was soft, whereas his proved he worked outside.

Dane refocused rather than go down the path of how well the two of them fit together. He needed to find a few bars for his cell phone. Eric might have already found a lead.

11

D ane located a small cave near the lake where he'd spent countless hours exploring as a kid. The only person who knew this area better than him was Jacob. Speaking of whom, Dane owed his friend a thank you. Without Eric to take point, Dane and Catalina wouldn't have had nearly as much time to escape the cabin. In their rush, a critical identifying piece of information might have been left behind. Jacob must've had a sixth sense after their conversation.

If the SUV driver ID'd Catalina, this place would most likely swarm with criminals. A guy like Kal Sutton would go all-in to protect his name, his company's reputation, and his freedom. He would lose all three if his plans came to light.

Dane would never understand folks who believed they could hide the truth. Eventually, everything done in darkness came to light. All the more reason the promise he'd made his father to keep a secret had been eating away at him for decades.

The suitcase fit into the small opening, as did his rucksack. Catalina gripped her backpack so hard her knuckles turned white.

"Mind if I hold onto this?" she asked.

"Be my guest." He gathered a few sticks and fallen branches to cover the mouth of the cave. He'd anticipated Catalina not wanting to part with her laptop. Wearing it as a backpack shouldn't slow her down and she could always give it to him if they needed to run. He was used to carrying three times the weight.

Once the luggage was secured, he reached for her hand. She met him halfway like the move was normal, automatic. The minute their fingers linked, the hum of electricity pulsed through him.

"What exactly did Kal Sutton say?" he asked, keeping his voice low as he led her toward the cabin using the long way around. There were no roads on the south side of the lake.

"That this app would give its owner an advantage like no other," she said. "They would be able to track Spec Ops soldiers and the government would never know what hit them."

"The military is becoming more surgical with attacks. Independent contractors are being used in many cases," he supplied. "What about those?"

"They could be followed as well." She shrugged. "It would probably even be easier."

"How long did Sutton think it would take for the US government to figure out what he was doing?" The intelligence community would have sniffed this out.

"He said something about it being applied strategically. That if this person overused it, he would be caught," she informed. "I have no idea who he was speaking to."

"What language did he speak in?" he asked.

"English," she confirmed.

"Did he use his regular voice or speak with any type of accent?" he continued.

"He did speak slower now that you mention it but no accent," she said.

"So, Sutton wants these guys to stay one step ahead of our Spec Ops. Interesting," he said, thinking about the damage this could cause.

"It would give them an unparalleled advantage," she agreed. "Imagine what they could get away with if they saw you guys coming or knew your location at all times."

"I don't want to live in a world where that is a reality, if I'm honest." He couldn't imagine having his every move tracked. The implications to soldiers were far reaching. There would be dozens of ways to manipulate the data to bring unfair advantage to the opposing side. Not to mention every soldier's life would be at the mercy of an enemy. It was anyone's guess what else the enemy would do with the data once it was in their hands.

"Sutton isn't getting anything now. But for how long? I can finish this code and sell it to Hanson, as planned. Once Kal Sutton knows it's possible, what's to stop him from hiring another person like me and going after this again?" She blinked a few times before she answered the question for herself. "Nothing. He'd have free reign."

"Which is why he needs to be caught and thrown in jail for the rest of his life where he can't betray his country. This is treason." Dane fisted his free hand thinking about it. Flexing a few times, he stopped and crouched down. He retrieved his cell from his back pocket and checked the screen. "Three bars."

12

T he coast is clear.
          Pls come home.
          Mom left Dad.

Those three messages from Eric caused Dane to issue a sharp sigh. He immediately texted his brother. *On my way.*

"I'm needed at the ranch." The thought his mother would ever walk out on his father was unimaginable, so he had to get home and see what this was really about. This most likely had to do with the recent revelation about Brax and not the secret Dane had been harboring. And yet, guilt assaulted him anyway. "I'd like to bring you with me."

"I didn't think going home was an option for you," she said, arching her brow.

Rather than explain, he showed her the screen of his cell.

Her face muscles relaxed when she read the first text. As she continued, her eyebrows drew together in concern. "Sounds serious."

"You don't know the half of it. This goes against every-thing she believes in," he said. "I need to go see for myself why she would do this after all these years, what the breaking point is and be there for her to show support."

Her gaze dropped to his free hand, and he realized he was fisting it. Yeah, a few of his demons reared their ugly heads. He had a good mind to tell his father what he really thought of him, as well as what he'd thought of the Marshall.

"Is there a place where I can be safely tucked away on property without anyone knowing I'm there?" she asked.

"I'd rather keep you close to me," he admitted. The thought of her being out of sight, vulnerable, raised his blood pressure. "Is that okay with you?"

She seemed to take her time thinking about it.

"As long as I can work on these last two bugs and finish the code without putting anyone else in jeopardy," she said.

"Let's head to my rental," he said. "Yours will most likely already be at the ranch."

"Won't people notice a random car?" she asked.

"Not at my family's ranch. People come and go all the time. Besides, we have top-notch security to keep anyone we don't want out." He searched her eyes for signs she was comfortable with the plan. "We could arrange to have your son brought there if that would help."

Her eyes lit up at the suggestion. She twisted her hands together. "It sounds too good to be true, even though it also sounds like heaven."

"But?" He picked up on a hesitation in her voice.

"I don't want him anywhere near this situation. Kal knows what my son looks like. He would make him a target. If we're together and he finds me, game over for both of us," she said, shaking her head. "I can't risk it."

"What if we bring him on the property but put him in someone else's care? We have multiple properties on the ranch, or I could even pass him off as my own son. No one would know the difference. Not even my family unless I told them otherwise." He figured she would think a whole lot clearer if she could take a break and peek in on her son. At the very least, she could relax a little bit knowing he was on the property and being well cared for.

"How would that play out with your family, Dane?" She looked at him with so much compassion in her eyes. "They seem to be going through quite a bit right now and your visit would be a complete surprise, coming out of nowhere. Plus, the thought of placing anyone else in the line of fire doesn't sit right with me. What if Kal shows?"

"Those are all realistic concerns, but my family is aware I'm making my way home," he said, thinking pawning her child off as his own had sounded a little too right. Dane dismissed the idea he could get attached to someone he hadn't even met yet. Although, he wasn't too far off doing the exact thing with Catalina. "I don't think there are any easy answers here. Only a menu of options with the least amount of pain."

"Moving him might be risky," she said.

"So is staying put. It's possible Kal or his people—and he would have people given everything at stake for him—could locate Luke anyway." He would feel better if he could keep eyes on the kid.

"He might have already staked out my grandmother's but that's where the trail ends," she said.

"He will dig into your background. He'll use social media. He'll have someone dig into your e-mail and possibly cell records in order to find you and your son," he said.

"How do you know?" she asked but seemed to already know the answer.

"Because it's what I would do," he said, guiding them to his rental car, ever aware there could be someone waiting, watching.

He opened the passenger door for her and then removed the branches he'd placed behind the vehicle the other night. It felt like he'd stashed the car here a week ago but it had only been two nights.

Catalina secured her seatbelt as he claimed the driver's seat. With the branches gone, he backed out of the spot and headed down the lane and toward the ranch.

"If you think it's safe to bring Luke to the ranch, I'd love to see my baby." Her tone of voice and the care in which she'd taken to make sure her son was safe meant she was an amazing mother. Lucky kid. Dane knew firsthand what it was like to have a mother who would trade her own happiness for her child's. It made keeping the secret all that much more horrendous. So much so, he'd blocked it out as a teenager. It resurfaced, though. That was the thing about inconvenient truths. They always cycled back around.

"Then, we'll figure out the best way to go about it once I know you're secured on the ranch," he reassured. If he had to extract her son by himself, he would do whatever it took to ease some of her pain and put a smile on her face.

"I have no idea what I did to deserve your kindness, Dane, but I'm grateful for it." She reached over and touched his arm, firing all kinds of electrical current through his body. The heat in the few kisses they'd shared imprinted his thoughts. He shook off the memory as best as he could. They couldn't afford another distraction. "And I'll figure out a way to repay you somehow."

"You don't owe me anything," he countered. "It's been a while since I felt useful. You're doing me a favor."

She shot a look of disbelief at him, but it was as true as Texas heat in August.

"Tell me everything you know about Kal Sutton," Dane said, figuring they could use the time it took to drive to the ranch productively. Plus, focusing on Sutton would keep Dane's thoughts on track and off Catalina.

"Personally?" she asked.

"The more I know everything about him, the better I'll be able to predict his behavior. If I can find the pattern, I'll know how to anticipate his moves," he explained.

"KAL GETS up and runs every morning at six a.m.," Catalina had worked for Kal Sutton going on four years. She'd been shocked to overhear his conversation and couldn't believe he would betray his country. "He's married. His wife is from Canada but grew up here in the States. They have two children, both girls, ages seven and nine."

"What about health concerns?" he asked.

"With his family? None as far as I know," she said. Didn't mean there weren't any.

"Financial concerns?" he asked.

"Again, nothing that he would share with me. I think his parents-in-law run an exporting business; they moved back to Vancouver sometime while their daughter was in college." She recognized the track he was on. He was looking for a reason, like medical bills or a sick child, for Kal to suddenly need an infusion of cash. It would make sense and certainly explain some of Kal's recent behavior. "He's close with her family so their business could be in trouble but don't quote me. From all appearances, they look solid."

Ideas were already clicking in Catalina's mind. Could

she hack into the system and check out his e-mail? She could get a sense of his relationship with his wife based on the way they communicated with each other. Was Kal in some kind of trouble? Trouble he couldn't find a way out of? It would make sense as to why he would have a need to sell the app to the highest bidder or someone he knew would pay big money for it.

"Other than a morning run, does he have any other rituals?" Dane asked. There was a whole lot of curiosity in his tone.

"He always left the office at six o'clock no matter what else was going on at work. Meetings could run over but he never failed to leave on time," she remembered. "On the rare occasion we had to stay later, he would return around eight p.m. I always figured he ate dinner with his family so I never asked about it."

"Would you classify his behavior as unusual lately?" Dane asked.

"He definitely kept his office door closed more but then he sometimes did that whenever a new government project was kicking off. He would keep quiet until he could discuss it with us." She shrugged. "I don't know what might have been happening while I was on maternity leave."

"Did he seem different when you came back to work? Moodier?"

"*Everything* seemed different. I figured out it was probably the fact I'd changed so much after having Luke," she admitted. "The funny thing is that I thought I'd have children *some*day way in the future when Lucas came home and got his mind right again. And then I lost Lucas before finding out I was pregnant with Luke. I was angry at first that he would never know his son. Lucas always wanted a boy and now he didn't even know he had a child. Now, I realize it all worked out the way it was supposed to. Lucas would have been even more miserable if he'd known he had a child on the way. Plus, I changed so much with the pregnancy."

"In what ways?"

"Climbing the ladder didn't appeal to me any longer. I wanted to put down roots somewhere and settle in." She shook her head. "If I'm completely honest, I wanted to stay home with Luke. He already lost his father and I didn't want him to be brought up by babysitters. I'd planned to ask Kal about the possibility of working from home at least a few days a week, but I'd been putting it off because he liked everyone at work and in the office. Face time was a big deal with him."

"And when you returned to work, you felt different so his changes didn't strike you as quite as odd as they might have," he said.

"He was taking more closed-door meetings," she admitted. "Like I said. Before. I didn't think too much about it. I did notice, though. Plus, he did seem different but, again, I chalked it up to me and not him. I think I even went in early one morning to reassure him I was committed to my job because I picked up on a vibe."

"What was his response?" he pressed.

"That he was happy to hear I was committed to the company and then he gave me this 'special project' to work on that had to stay under wraps," she said.

"What about everyone else in the office?" he asked. "Co-workers? Admins?"

"I worked with a lot of men in my department. Some made it pretty clear they thought I got the job because I was a woman, and I overheard someone crack they wished they got six weeks of vacation just for having a baby," she said.

"They sound like real jerks," Dane said.

"They played basketball together at lunch and I never got the invite," she said. Thinking back, her time at the company had been lonely. Of course, she had Lucas and he made it known he didn't like her working around so many guys. "Lucas didn't like it anyway."

Dane gripped the steering wheel a little bit tighter. He seemed to debate whether or not he was going to say what was on his mind.

She waited until he decided.

"You are the most loyal and devoted person I've met in a long time," he finally said. "The last thing anyone in a relationship with you should question is your devotion."

"Lucas didn't see it that way." Hearing it from Dane was refreshing. She'd gotten a little too used to being questioned. "Being so far away seemed to make him insecure."

"He should have done a better job. You deserve to be trusted," Dane said and it seemed like there was more on his mind that he decided to keep to himself.

It was the same thought she'd had countless times, despite understanding Lucas wasn't quite himself and hadn't been for quite some time.

"Despite recent actions, Kal has never struck me as the kind of person who would betray something like this, Dane." She changed the subject, not wanting to talk about her relationship with Lucas in the final years. She'd rather remember the bright, vibrant kid from Oklahoma who'd made her feel at home on the first day she transferred to a new school.

"He might not have a choice. A desperate person is a dangerous person," he said as he turned onto a private road.

When Dane said the ranch had security, she wasn't sure what she'd envisioned. A guy who patrolled the house on foot. Or someone who drove around on a golf cart, checking each of the homes. She sure didn't expect to pull up to a guard shack with two security officers inside and who knew how many more out on the property. The idea of bringing Luke here made more sense now that she saw firsthand what the coverage would be like.

Again, she couldn't imagine having the kind of money and resources that would require this much security. She realized being part of a wealthy cattle ranch family could potentially put a target on Dane's back. Being here could also distort a person's reality. Then again, he was one of the most down to earth people she'd ever met. Nothing about him screamed money from his t-shirt to jeans and boots. His low-key demeanor and outlook that was grounded in reality added to his charm.

Security waved and raised the gate the minute he got a good look at the driver. The guard's face morphed to shock and he tried to recover quickly.

Massive was the best way to describe the main house. And beautiful. Being here and surrounded by so much... *everything*...would make Catalina feel out of place were it not for the person in the driver's seat. There was something comforting about being with Dane, like the world was righted again, spinning on its axis just the way it was designed to do.

Her heart skipped at the thought of bringing Luke here. The only fear at this point was the possibility of something happening before someone could get to him or while he was on his way. And yet, having him close by would ease her panic levels.

Fixing the bugs and finishing the code so she could put this whole mess behind her and start her life anew with her son was never a bigger priority.

She thought about her discussion with Dane on the way over. Was Kal under the gun? Was there a way to find out? She knew the name of the export company his in-laws owned. She could do a little digging around.

Besides, it occurred to her that if Kal was going to mess with her family, there were ways she could mess with his. Now, she was starting to think.

"I know Kal's address," she said. "I can walk his block via the Web and see if he has any security set up. If he has a camera or security system, I can most likely hack into it."

"That could give us some valuable information as to what he might be up to," Dane said.

"I don't know why I didn't think of it before," she stated. "All I need is proof he's up to something to get the DA interested, right?"

"That's one way to go about it," Dane said.

She realized soldiers had a different, more direct way of handling a threat. Going at it face-to-face sure would be easier. Except that she knew it didn't quite always go down like that overseas. There were times when a soldier had to stand his ground and practically take a bullet because the government was pulling strings or had a political agenda that didn't mesh with a direct attack.

Could she get answers by taking a different approach?

13

D ane parked next to the house, readying himself to face everyone inside. Eric came out of the house, making his way toward the rental sedan. Catalina's vehicle was there, already parked in the lot as expected. Dane had no intention of asking how it got there.

"Thanks for coming, Dane," Eric said after greeting Catalina. "Mom isn't herself, except when she's with Angel. Otherwise, she's crying and seems miserable."

"Has he been here?"

They both knew he referred to their father.

"Yes. For what it's worth, she's refusing to let him in the house," Eric said.

"Did she say why?" Dane feared the worst.

"She said there've been too many secrets and she can't take it any longer," Eric supplied.

"Did she elaborate?" Dane's gut twisted in a knot. Had she found out about his?

"She's mentioned the situation with Brax a few times," Eric said. "But it feels like there has to be more to it than that."

"Are more of us half brothers?" The question came out before he could reel it back in. He shot a look of apology. "Just to be clear, Brax isn't half anything to me. He's one hundred percent my brother."

Guilt slammed into him at being away from the family for so long, and for keeping his father's secret. It had been a little too easy to cut himself off from home and all the drama when he was overseas.

"We all feel the exact same," Eric said. "And we all looked at each other with the same question."

"Catalina needs a quiet corner to work in, and I'd like to talk to you about a mission involving bringing a baby to the ranch," Dane said, placing a hand on his brother's shoulder.

Eric shot a quizzical look, but he didn't say anything. Instead, he nodded, seeming to realize information was better off on a need-to-know basis.

"You know you can count on me and any one of the others. Let us know what you need and when you need it, brother," Eric said.

"What about our cousins? Do you have a relationship with them anymore?" Dane couldn't help but ask. So far, Eric had only spoken about this branch of the family tree.

"Like I said, the family has been messed up for a while," Eric said. "Folks picked sides."

"Shame," Dane said.

"I know," Eric agreed. His gaze bounced from Dane to Catalina and back. "Are you ready to go inside?"

The comradery between brothers was something Dane had missed dearly. He was just beginning to realize how much he missed his brothers. Closing off to them, to his family, hadn't made the pain go away. Instead, he'd withdrawn from everyone he loved. The realization struck like a physical blow. Holding in his father's secret had eaten Dane alive from the inside out. He could see the toll it had taken. Dane didn't want to keep secrets any longer. Could he deliver the blow to his mother while she was already down if she didn't already know?

The dilemma was real. Dane didn't care what happened to his father at this point. The man deserved whatever he got as far as Dane was concerned. Dane had kept the secret for his mother's sake, not his father's. And the only question now in his mind was when would be the right time to tell her. Because this thing had destroyed Dane's relationships with his family, and he couldn't allow that to happen any longer.

Gravel spewed underneath tires as a vehicle sped around from the back of the house. The noise stopped Dane midway between the sedan and the front door. The truck that came roaring from around the side of the building belonged to Dane's father.

"Do you mind taking Catalina inside and setting her up in one of the bedrooms?" Dane asked his brother.

"Will you be all right out here with him?" Eric seemed to pick up on the tension.

"I will," Dane countered. "Not so sure about him."

Catalina's hand on Dane's arm grounded him. Her lightest touch reminded him to keep the past in the rearview.

"I can stay if you'd like," Catalina said, and her voice was filled with compassion.

"No need," he reassured, turning to her. Dane dipped his head down and pressed a kiss to her pink lips. He needed that more than air. "Go on inside and get set up. I'll be there as soon as I can. Okay?"

Catalina's smile would convince a death row inmate everything would work out fine.

"I'll wait for you," she said, pushing up to her tiptoes to kiss him one more time.

"This won't take long," he reassured.

Eric led her toward the front door as Brodie Firebrand brought his truck into a screeching halt. By the time Catalina disappeared inside, Dane's father was exiting his vehicle.

Dane charged his father like a bull in front of a waving red flag. He threw his elbow into his father's chest and backed him up against the truck, staring the man in the eyes the whole time.

"I'm not nine years old any longer, and I won't keep your secrets anymore," Dane managed to grind out despite clenching his back teeth.

Eyes wide, mouth agape, his father didn't seem able to hide his shock.

"Is that what this is about? Is that why you took off and barely looked back?" His father asked.

"That's none of your business," Dane stated.

"It is, though," his father said. "Because your mother has been worried sick all these years, wondering what she did wrong, and I'm just now finding out it was my fault."

"She wouldn't hurt a soul," he countered. "Exactly the reason I couldn't break her heart."

"You plan to tell her everything?" His father asked, a mix of shame and regret passed behind his blue eyes. Those weren't emotions Dane wanted to see or acknowledge in his father. What he had to do would be much easier if the man was a heartless monster—a monster Dane had convinced himself existed far too many years to go back now.

"No."

His father's eyebrow shot up in confusion.

"I won't have to," Dane said.

The man really looked confused now.

"You will." Dane couldn't be any clearer than that. "If I have to force you myself."

"She'll leave me permanently this time," his father said.

"Then you deserve to be alone because the woman inside this house," he pointed, "deserves a man who will love her *and* be faithful."

"I have been," his father said. "I admit to being a jerk in the early years of our marriage but ever since you...ever since the day out camping that you...it changed me."

His father broke eye contact as emotion seemed to be getting the best of him.

"What changed you?" Dane asked, not ready to let it go. "Getting caught?"

"Seeing the look in your eyes. It made me wake up and realize what I'd become, and I didn't like it," he said.

"You don't seem to have done a great job of convincing Mom to stay with you." Dane's words came out angry. One admission, despite the honesty in his father's eyes, did not make up for all the years of suffering. Dane wasn't ready to forgive his father yet. There was no 'on' or 'off' button when it came to emotions. And, honestly, he might never be able to forgive the man.

His father hung his head. "No, I haven't."

"Then, why should I care about you?" he asked.

"I don't deserve your forgiveness. I don't deserve to be the father of any one of you. It's not my place to say, but you've all turned out to be men I'm proud to call my sons," he said.

"Despite the fact you don't deserve the credit?" Dane couldn't stop himself.

"Never said I did. Your mom does, though," he said.

Dane bit back a few swear words—words he would

freely use if not for the upbringing his mother had provided that taught him to respect his elders. It was for her and her alone that Dane didn't really give his father a piece of his mind.

As it was, he'd said all he was going to.

"If you'll convince your mother to give me a chance to speak to her, I'll tell her everything, Dane. I swear."

Dane released his hold on his father. The man who'd once been Dane's idol and a tower of strength, didn't look so big now.

"I'm nothing without her," he pleaded. "And I spent the past twenty-plus years trying to deserve her. I don't. That's no secret."

"Yeah? Maybe you shouldn't have had secrets from her in the first place. You should have treated her the way she deserved to be treated. Then, you wouldn't be in this mess," Dane ground out. "I kept your secret. You have to figure out a way to get her to speak to you on your own. I'm done with you."

With that, Dane turned and walked inside the house. He half expected his father to follow him. When he didn't, Dane turned around. From the window, he saw his father's shoulders slump forward as he climbed inside his truck. Head down, he looked defeated.

Dane cursed the fact he'd looked back. He couldn't afford to feel sorry for his father.

On a sharp sigh, he followed the sound of voices toward the kitchen. The main living room to his right had been transformed into a magical-looking playroom. The floors were covered with bright squares that connected like puzzle pieces. There was a tee-pee in one corner and more toys than a kid could ever play with scattered around the room. The flooring looked soft and spongy. He thought Catalina's son might like to play in a room like this one.

Why was his first thought about Catalina's kid?

Rather than examine the question, he faced the kitchen and didn't stop walking until he reached it. The place was much like he remembered, a chef's dream. The large island centered the room and a long wooden table sat to his left with enough chairs to seat an army of men.

The minute he set foot inside the room he heard a gasp. His attention shifted toward the sound. His mother bounded up from her seat, handed over a baby who must be Angel, and barreled toward him. She was five feet two on a good day, but like a bullet when she ran into him with her arms out. She threw her arms around his midsection and cried.

He stood there, hugging the woman who'd been his rock, realizing how hard his absence must have been on her. Wow, a realization struck. He'd been a huge jerk when it came to his mother's feelings. Why was it so easy to take loved ones for granted?

Was he any better than his father? His mind mounted an immediate response to the question because he hadn't broken wedding vows, but he was beginning to see how much he'd neglected her feelings.

Not wanting to be in the same room as her for all these years through no fault of her own was a gut punch and a reality check. Dane needed to do better. His mother deserved better. And, no, he wouldn't tell her the secret he'd been keeping. He had every intention of standing by while his father explained everything. But right now, he just wanted to reassure his mom.

"I can't believe you're here," she finally said before looking up at him with red-rimmed eyes. She made a show of touching his arm, reaching up to cup his cheeks before tweaking one. She blinked a couple of times before a wide smile broke out. His mother was still beautiful, despite her age-worn skin. The vibrancy in her eyes was dimmer, and he suspected it had to do with leaving her husband. That wasn't a decision she'd take lightly by any means. And then it seemed to dawn on her. She shook her head. "If you're going to try to talk me into going back home. Forget it."

She turned her back toward him.

"I will do no such thing," He reached up and placed his hands on her shoulders. "I came home strictly for your meatballs."

She spun around. The smile had returned.

"Now, you're talking." She clapped her hands together. "I have a fresh batch in the fridge."

He would try to talk her out of heating up a plate but had no plans to insult her like that. While she gaited toward the fridge, he moved to the table where Eric sat talking with Adam. There was another new face at the table, and he assumed it belonged to Prudence. His sister-in-law? Now, there was a weird thought.

Adam stood up the minute Dane got close. He introduced Dane to his wife before bringing him into a bear hug. Dane had to admit, seeing his brother face to face was nicer than he'd imagined it would be. Being home was nice. He'd said his piece with his father and a weight he didn't realize he'd been carrying around with him all these years lifted. He stepped lighter and felt a sense of freedom he hadn't experienced at this ranch since he was a kid. There was a lot to be said for confronting his demons.

"I hear you have a daughter," he said to Adam. "This must be her."

Adam practically beamed. There was something

different about him and Dane figured it had to do with the two ladies at the table, Prudence and Angel.

"She's beautiful," Dane said. It was true. He'd never been much of a baby person but this was different. There was something special about Angel, and he had no idea what the change was about. Family?

"That kid has our hearts in her little fist," Adam admitted. There was something different about him too. His outer shell was still a reminder he was strong as an ox, but his softer side came out, and the smile on his face and love in his eyes could best be described as at peace.

What was that like?

"Hey, man," Adam said, lowering his voice. "What about you? You brought a friend here?"

"Catalina Ivey. I hope that's okay," Dane said.

"Of course," Adam waved like it was no big deal. "We had some trouble here at the main house recently, so I have to ask if everything's okay."

"As a matter of fact, it isn't." Dane gave a quick rundown of Catalina's situation and the status of her son. "I have no idea where he is but I'd like to bring him here for safety's sake. Plus, I think Catalina will be able to concentrate better with him nearby. As it is, she keeps checking the time and reaching for her phone before setting it down again."

"Her instincts are to check on her baby," Prudence stated.

"That's what I was thinking too," Dane said. Prudence reassured him that he was on the right track. "She didn't want to come here because she's concerned about placing everyone in danger."

"We understand the risks," Adam said. "And we'll put everything on the line for family."

Warmth spread through Dane's chest at hearing those

words, the reassurance. "It means a lot to hear you say that, Adam."

"You'd do the same for me, right?"

"I should have been here and I would have. Eric filled me in." Dane shook his head. "I'm sorry for letting you down."

"You didn't do anything of the kind," Adam quickly admonished. "We all have a path, and we all have to figure out what that is and what it means. I know without a shadow of a doubt that if I'd told you what was going on you would have been on the first plane."

Dane was already rocking his head before his brother finished his sentence.

"I've never doubted your family is your priority," Adam said.

"I haven't shown it nearly enough," Dane said. "And that changes now."

"What's the plan to bring the kid here?" Adam asked, reclaiming his seat and motioning for Dane to sit down.

Prudence excused herself after handing the baby over to Adam. It was quite a sight to see Adam cradling his daughter in his arms. The image hit Dane full force. Right behind it came an image of him, Luke, and Catalina as a family. The toothless smile he'd seen on her laptop when she thought he wasn't looking had touched his heart.

Didn't that just throw a curveball into Dane's plan to be single for the rest of his natural life?

14

———

"I haven't come up with a plan as of yet. The idea is still taking shape." Dane decided this wasn't the time to analyze his future, so he shook off the image of him, Catalina, and her son as one family best as he could. Clasping his hands, he placed them on the table. The smell of home wafted through the kitchen as his mother heated up her signature dish, meatballs. It was a shame the Marshall didn't open his home up to family meals while he was alive.

"Gotcha. We'll think on it some more," Adam said as their mother brought over a plate.

"I hear you moved into the main house. What's going on?" Dane asked her. She set the plate down without making eye contact, grunting disapproval at the change of topic.

"Too many secrets. Too many lies," she said, throwing her hands in the air. It was a good thing she waited to set the plates down before responding. The woman had a habit of talking with her hands. The more emotion behind the words, the bigger the gestures.

Guilt stabbed him in the center of the chest. He hated secrets and part of him wanted to speak up. Wasn't his place. Besides, he assumed she was talking about Brax since she wasn't giving Dane the evil eye he deserved. Realization dawned that he never should have held onto this secret for so long. He didn't deserve the forgiveness she would give him.

"Do you know?" she asked, and the look of pain in her eyes nearly gutted him.

He nodded.

"He's my son in every sense of the word," she continued without flinching. Of course she would. No one had sensed Brax being treated differently while growing up.

"Explains why he was always your favorite." Dane kept a serious face as he looked at his mother for all of two seconds before he broke into laughter.

She laughed too, and it was the first time she seemed to exhale around him.

"You did what you believed was right," he reassured.

"Did I?" Her question hit home. "How many times could I have told him? Too many. But I chose not to and now he's hurting. It's a mother's job to protect her children."

"Which is what you thought you were doing," Dane reminded her.

"By lying? How will he ever trust me again?" For the second time, a question hit a little too close to home and he thought about breaking his silence.

His father had better come clean soon. Dane doubted he'd be able to keep the secret much longer.

"Can I ask a personal question?" he started.

She nodded but her smile faded.

"Did you forgive him?" he asked.

"It took a long time," she admitted. Her discomfort with the subject was obvious and he got his answer. Would dredging up the past only cause more pain?

"I have a friend with me," Dane changed the subject. "She's probably starving. I'd like to take—"

Mother waved him off and Eric stood up, volunteering to take Catalina a plate.

"Why isn't she down here with us?" Mother asked.

"She has important work to do," he said. Not a lie. And he was grateful his mother seemed content to let it go at that.

"Everyone needs to eat," Mother said. What was it about mothers that had them wanting to feed everyone all the time?

"I hear the family is going through a rough patch since the Marshall's passing." Again, Dane changed the subject. The less he told everyone about Catalina, the better for everyone all the way around, and for her. Although, part of him wanted his family to get to know her better. No matter what else happened once this was over, he wanted to be part of her and Luke's lives. Like an uncle. He owed Lucas that much. Once he put the word out to the other guys from their unit, they would want to be part of Luke's upbringing too. Catalina said her grandmother was the only family she had left. That had just changed. Lucas was about to gain a few uncles.

Then, there was Dane's family to consider. Closing himself off from his brothers was one of many regrets. Had he bottled everything up inside? Believed he had to take on the world by himself?

Dane had always preferred being alone out on the property, but he was also starting to realize that being forced to hold in his father's secret had caused Dane to pull away from the family at an early age. He'd gone inside himself, taken the world on his shoulders. He was beginning to see it so clearly now.

Some of the anger he'd been holding inside was abating. He was beginning to get a clearer picture of why he'd felt the need to push away everyone and everything he loved.

Kids had a way of convincing themselves everything that happened was their fault. Dane was guilty. But that was changing.

"Dad and Uncle Keif have never been at each other's throats more," Adam spoke up. "It's awful."

"I hear Uncle Keif stuck his nose where it doesn't belong. That couldn't have helped," Dane said.

"True. He was arrested and could have been sent away for a while after Ed Roberts' murder," Adam supplied. "But Corbin and Liv's relationship is just the current excuse for an all-out war between the families."

"Don't people ever get tired of this fighting?" Dane asked.

"You already know how I feel about Kellan. But, yes, I agree with what you're saying," Adam said. "Looks like the clause in the Marshall's will might have to be invoked to solve the dispute."

"What clause?"

"You haven't heard?" Adam's eyebrow shot up.

Dane shook his head.

"If their sons end up married before Dad and Uncle Keif can come to an agreement, the inheritance skips a generation and everything is evenly divided among us," Adam informed.

"That's the way it should have been in the first place if

you ask me," Mother said. "We should all be working together anyway."

"But that means you'd have to get closer to Aunt Jackie," Adam teased.

Their mother drew in a sharp breath and threw her hands in the air.

The sounds of boots shuffling down the hallway, broke into the conversation. Dad appeared at the doorway with a fistful of wildflowers. He stopped before entering, his gaze searching for Mother.

She froze for a few seconds, and then waved her arms in the air. "No. No. No."

"You need to hear something, Lucia," he said. "And you need to hear it from me. There were others all those years ago. I stopped just like I promised." His gaze shot to from his wife to Dane and back. "I forced one of our children to keep my secret when I got caught and I doubt he'll ever forgive me for it."

"You don't deserve it." Shaking her head, she scurried out the back door.

Neither Adam nor Dane invited their dad inside. Too much bad blood. The man hadn't made an attempt to get close to any of his sons, so it was no surprise to Dane that Adam seemed to feel the same way toward the man.

No one told him to leave either. He'd said his piece and there was no reason for him to stick around.

Eric entered the room. His gaze moving over the scene, taking in the strange silence.

"I shouldn't have come, but she needed to know," their father said before turning and walking back down the same hallway from where he came a few uncomfortable moments ago.

As far as Dane saw, it wasn't their job to make the man

they barely knew comfortable. If he wanted to truly prove he'd changed, he was going to have to make the effort with them. At least, he had taken the first step by coming clean to Dane's mother. It mattered.

"What was that all about?" Eric asked as he reclaimed his spot at the table.

Dane shrugged.

"Your guess is as good as ours," Adam said.

"I have a friend upstairs who needs protection," Dane said. "We all know that part. She has a kid around the same age as Angel who is tucked away. We need to get him here safely without drawing attention."

"Always sounds easier than it is," Adam said.

"I know you've been through a lot," Dane said to his brother. "I wouldn't blame you for tapping out of this mission."

"That's not how we work around here and you should know it." There was a twinge of frustration in Adam's voice. Frustration that was not only reasonable but deserved an explanation. Adam put his hand up to stop Dane from speaking. "I'm just happy you're here, brother. Don't listen to everything I say. Okay?"

"I deserved it and so much more." Dane's admission elicited quite a look from his brother. "Something happened that I can't tell you about just yet. Someone else deserves to hear it first—"

"Hear what?" Corbin walked into the kitchen. His gaze widened when it landed on Dane. "I thought I recognized the voice but decided I was probably hallucinating." He made a show of blinking a few times. "Is it really you, Dane Firebrand?"

Dane took the comments in stride. He was owed that and more as far as he was concerned after ditching the family the way he did. Instead of answering, he stood up, crossed the room, and brought his brother into a hug.

"I've missed you," Corbin said quietly, the emotion in his voice struck a chord with Dane.

"Same here. I want to be a better brother," Dane said.

"You came to the right place," Corbin teased, lightening the moment happening between them.

"Good. Because you're stuck with me now," Dane teased right back, walking beside his brother to the table.

"Mom's meatballs," Corbin said, patting his belly. "I've put on a few pounds thanks to those."

"I'd forgotten how great they were," Dane admitted.

"Now, that's a real shame," Adam piped in.

It was good to be home, surrounded by his brothers. But he needed to check on his mother before coming up with a plan to get Luke here. "Think it's a bad sign Mom's not back yet?"

"Sit down," Corbin said. "I can go check on her. She was out back a minute ago."

He walked over to the window.

"Well..." He looked around, moving from window to window. "I don't know where she took off to."

"I'll try to get her on her cell phone," Adam piped in. He located his and then palmed it. He made a call, tapping his fingers on the table while waiting for a response. "Nothing. I guess she isn't ready to speak to anyone just yet."

"What happened?" Corbin asked.

"Dad," came Dane's quick response.

"Oh." Corbin smacked his hand on the table. "What did he do now?"

"Showed up with flowers and made another confession," Adam supplied.

Dane was beginning to feel a twinge of guilt there. He'd

been a jerk to his brothers, essentially cutting them out of his life for years and the first three he encountered forgave him instantly. Granted, his father had messed up on a very different scale. However, how could Dane accept his brothers' forgiveness while he was still condemning his father for mistakes he made in the past? It didn't jive despite the difference in magnitude. Mistakes were mistakes no matter the size. A little voice inside his head argued the opposite was true, that scale mattered. Maybe it did. But Dane wouldn't be able to truly move on until he forgave his father.

"I'll be back in a little while." He looked to Eric. "Can you check on Catalina and see if she needs anything? Tell her I'll be on property thinking up a plan for Luke but there's something I have to do in the meantime."

"Done," Eric said and Dane believed him.

He thanked his brother before heading out the front door, hoping his father had gone either to the barn or home. He stopped in his tracks the minute he stepped onto the porch. His father was inside the truck, engine running, slumped forward like he'd gone to sleep. Something felt very off.

Dane bolted toward the truck and reached the driver's side in a matter of seconds. His father looked like he was sleeping. Not a good sign.

Dane opened the door, thankful it wasn't locked.

"Dad," he said, placing his hand on his father's shoulder. The man didn't move.

"Dad." Dane raised his voice this time before reaching over and shutting off the engine. The flowers were all over the seat and floorboard as though he'd dropped them.

Dane shook his father. His head rolled from side to front like his neck was broken. Palming his cell, he called 911, and requested an ambulance. His next call was to Eric. "There's something wrong with Dad." He skimmed his father, searching for signs he'd been knocked out. And then he checked for a pulse. Got one, but it was weak. "I think Dad might have had a heart attack."

More of that guilt surfaced, but there was no time to deal. Dane pocketed his cell and eased the seat back in the truck. He unbuttoned his father's shirt, giving the older man space to breathe.

"I know we've had our differences, but you can't die on me. Not now. You need to live and make this right with your family, not like the Marshall. Look at what he did. Look at the mess he left behind." Dane heard the rush of feet moving toward him. He backed up a couple of steps to give his father room to breathe as the others circled around.

"Is he breathing?" Adam said.

"Yes. He has a pulse but it's weak," Dane stated. "Someone go get an aspirin in case he comes to."

"Got it," Corbin said before taking off toward the house.

"Still, it's a pulse. That's good." Adam held up his phone. "I'll try Mom again."

Dane nodded. Out of the corner of his eye, he saw Catalina come rushing over. He stepped back and out of the fray. Rather than speak, he gathered her in his arms. "It's my dad. I think he's had a heart attack."

"I'm sorry, Dane." She hooked her arms around him and pressed her cheek against his chest as they waited for an ambulance.

It seemed to take forever but was more like twenty minutes.

As a pair of EMTs came running toward them, the group disbursed, and Dane's mother came running from the back of the house. Adam saw her at the same time as her mouth dropped. He started toward her, telling everyone he had this.

"I'm so sorry, Dane," Catalina whispered as one of the EMTs ran to the back of the ambulance and returned with a gurney.

By the time his father was removed from the truck, he had an oxygen mask secured over his nose and mouth. He didn't so much as blink as the EMTs moved him onto the gurney or attempt to move in any way. The thought of losing him while they had unfinished business between them sat hard on Dane's chest.

"We're taking him to Lone Star Pass General," one of the EMTs said as he rolled on past.

"Thank you." Dane didn't recognize him, but his nametag read: Sebastian.

"I need to see my husband." Mother's concern was written in the deep lines in her forehead and her frown.

The EMTs stopped for a few seconds.

"We're losing time, ma'am," Sebastian said.

"Go on," she said, looking more than a little bit lost. She wrung her hands together.

"I've got Mom," Adam said. "We'll follow the ambulance in Dad's truck."

The keys were still in the ignition. The others promised to meet them there.

"Take care of her," Dane said to his brother. He couldn't leave the ranch. Relocating Catalina's son just got shoved back. There was no way he would risk a mission like that one without his brothers' help.

"I will," Adam said. He motioned toward the house. "Take care of mine while I'm gone."

"You know it. Now, go." Dane linked his hand with

Catalina's as they moved to the porch to get out of the truck's way.

Eric stayed back but Corbin hopped in the back seat of the truck before it pulled out.

"Too much death going on around here," Eric said quietly.

Dane hoped they wouldn't be adding his father to the count.

15

C atalina sat at the kitchen table, fingers on her laptop as Dane paced along with his brother Eric. The temptation to check on Luke was a force unto itself. She had to fight the urge to reach out to her babysitter. This was a big risk, and she didn't want to do anything to jeopardize the sitter, or her and Luke's location. Catalina needed to be patient a little bit longer.

Not knowing how her baby was doing, though, was eating away at her. Catalina had given the friend of her grandmother's a number to call in case of a dire emergency. Her instructions had been strict, life or death only. She couldn't risk Kal intercepting the call. He didn't have the skills to tap her phone, but he could get someone on her old team to do it. Others would have the ability. Plus, he might have hired creeps to find her. For all she knew, there could be a bounty on her head.

Time was ticking by, and she hadn't heard her son's laugh in far too many days now. Her arms literally ached to hold him. A necessary sacrifice. Not an easy one, though.

Catalina's fingers danced across the keyboard. The work-around for another bug was coming to her. All she needed to do now was test it. And...

Yes. Progress. It worked.

One more to go and then all she needed to do was finish writing the code. She was close. She could feel it. Although, selling it to Hanson Tech for a profit was losing its appeal. The question remained...should anyone own a program like this? Was there a better answer? Scrap the project altogether, and what? Wait for someone else to develop it?

Catalina tapped her finger on the wooden table. There had to be a way to stop this from ever being developed. Right?

Could development be blocked legally? What would happen after she finished this app? What would Hanson do with it? Sell it to the US? Use it to strengthen their partnership with the government? She could live with the last part, except the bit about Kal getting off scot-free.

Selling the app to Hanson gave Kal a get-out-of-jail-free card, didn't it? As much as she couldn't imagine her boss in bed with an enemy nation, he needed to be locked away for the attempt. Catalina thought about the man's wife and kids. She'd met them at company picnics. They seemed like a normal family. But then, wasn't that exactly how people got away with spying and treason? Wasn't it always the one people least expected?

Better yet, could she dig up information about Kal and his family? What about his wife's family and their export business?

Catalina pulled up a search engine and engaged spy mode, an app that allowed her to search without anyone being able to track her movements on the Web. What was the name of Charlotte Sutton's family company? Maybe she could just search for the name and see if she was listed. Nope. Nothing. Too easy.

What else? An idea came to her. She could check the woman's social media accounts. Catalina pulled up the most popular family and friends site. Bingo. Charlotte had a page where she shared pictures of her family, and a trip home last summer. Hold on a second...

Yes. There it was. Charlotte standing with her father in front of a warehouse with the name Tremblay Exports. It only took Catalina sixty seconds to find out Tremblay Exports was in debt once she had a name.

Needing money to bail out Charlotte's family would be a good reason to sell an app to an enemy country.

She looked over at Dane and the minute their gazes locked, he started toward her. He seemed to know she'd found something without her needing to say the words.

"What is it?" he asked, standing behind her. He leaned forward, placing one hand on the table and another on the back of her chair. She could breathe in his spicy scent with him this close.

Catalina cleared her throat and gave herself a mental headshake.

"Tremblay Exports is in trouble." She pointed to the business journal article. "The company is on the verge of financial ruin and needs a cash infusion to keep it going."

"Let me guess what Kal Sutton's wife's maiden name is," Dane said.

"You'd be right," Catalina confirmed. "It makes more sense to me that Kal would do anything to protect his wife than him being out to hurt his own country—a country he loves."

"It's a desperate act," he said. "And would explain his different behavior when you returned to work."

She nodded.

"Look at this." She pulled up Charlotte's social media page. "I do realize you can't exactly believe everything on social media. People only put their best foot forward and it becomes more of a brag fest for some. However, this family looks truly happy to me."

Dane seemed to agree. He issued a sharp sigh. "When a man's back is against a wall and his family hangs in the balance, he might not make the right decisions."

"Kal might not think he has another choice," she admitted. Looking at the faces of his children, she couldn't help but think she would do anything she could to protect her own. Of course, she couldn't see herself breaking the law. There was always another way if someone looked hard enough. And now Kal was going to end up in jail for the rest of his life. How vulnerable would his family be then? Tremblay Exports would be in financial ruin and Kal's assets would be frozen. He clearly hadn't thought this through.

But then desperate times called for desperate measures. One question remained...how desperate was Kal and how far was he willing to go to keep his secrets?

DANE FISTED HIS HANDS. Granted, he didn't have a family to support so he didn't feel right judging Kal Sutton. Except the man wasn't thinking long game. Which meant more than just the Tremblay family's fortune was at stake.

Had someone threatened Kal? His wife? His children? The money might be necessary to make a different kind of threat go away. Either way, Kal had made the wrong choice. What did he think? He could use his company's talent to write and sell an app that would, in turn, harm the military men and women keeping him safe? The move smelled of desperation and there had to be more than just money involved.

Of course, Dane had the distinct advantage of having more zeroes in his bank account than he could ever use or need. He preferred a simple life to throwing money around. And, yet there he was surrounded by secrets anyway—secrets that were finally coming to light.

Now that his dad was in the hospital, Dane had to hold off telling his mom what had happened. And yet, the secret was literally eating a hole in his stomach. Dane glanced over at Eric, who'd made his umpteenth trip around the kitchen. He could confide in his brother. And yet, all he really wanted to do was tell Catalina.

"Families have secrets, even from each other," Dane started in little more than a whisper.

"Yeah?" Catalina said, leaning back and folding her arms across her chest. "Do you want to tell me about them?"

Dane came around to take a seat beside her. He looked into those cornflower blue eyes of hers and wanted to tell her all his secrets.

"The reason I left Lone Star Pass was because I'd been forced to keep a secret from my family, my mother," he said.

There was no judgment in Catalina's eyes, only compassion.

"My father took me out to hunt poachers when I was nine years old. My mother said I was too young to go and that my father should take one of the older boys, but he refused," Dane continued. Guilt stabbed him at the memory. "I thought it was because he wanted to bond with me. My nine-year-old brain that desperately wanted a relationship with my father decided this was it. He chose me because I was special to him." He flashed eyes at her. "I was a naïve kid."

"No, you weren't," she quickly defended, fire in her eyes. "It's not naïve to want your parents to love you. I think it's one of the most basic human needs there is."

She might be right but that didn't dull the pain at his own foolishness.

"Anyway, he clearly had other ideas. We followed a trail but he didn't say two words to me the entire time. He set up two tents on opposite sides of a campfire that he'd built. Ordered me to go in one of the tents and not come out unless it was on fire," he said. Anger fisted his hands. He flexed and released his fingers to work out some of the tension.

Catalina reached over and took one of his hands in hers, clasping their fingers.

"A few hours later, I hear what I think is my dad wrestling with a bear or some wild animal. I'd never heard those sounds from humans before. So, I think this is my chance to win his love. I'll save him from whatever is in there, fighting him." Embarrassment caused anger to rip through him. "I grabbed my Beretta and headed for the tent. I'm quiet as I unzip the zipper. It never occurs to me that it shouldn't be zipped in the first place. My nerves are through the roof, my hands are shaking, but I force calm."

Flashes of memories assault him.

"The covers are over both of them, so I can't see what he's fighting against but it looks to me like I'm going to lose my dad."

"I'm sorry." Catalina's quiet words were balm to his wounded soul.

"I shout for my dad and whatever is on top of him gets knocked off, so I shoot," he said. "There's blood everywhere and he's shouting at me, calling me all kinds of names. I'm confused, though, because I still think I just saved his life."

At some point, Eric has taken a seat at the table, but Dane didn't notice when.

Catalina's beautiful face morphs into a frown.

"Dad starts shouting at me and all I do is run away. I panicked but I remember the face of the woman who'd been on top of dad because she was our fourth grade teacher, Mrs. Maples," he said. "I'm lost in the woods for days. There's blood splatter on my clothes and I'm surviving on a base level."

"You were gone for three days to be exact," Eric said quietly as he joined them. "We were all searching for you, losing our minds."

"By the time I was found, I think I blocked most of it out," Dane admitted. "Dad and the Marshall were there. They said what really happened could never be spoken about again. They said I had to go along with their version of the events or spend the rest of my life behind bars."

"Mrs. Maples isn't dead," Eric said, sounding confused.

"What? She has to be. I killed her. Dad and the Marshall covered it up," Dane said.

"No." Eric shook his head. "She moved to Houston after a hunting accident shattered her leg."

"How can that be?" Dane gave himself a mental head-shake. "I saw the blood."

"Did you see a body?" Eric asked.

"No...but..."

Dane's memories were foggy at best but he'd been so sure that he'd killed her.

"Dad and the Marshall let you believe that so you wouldn't tell Mom about the affair. Plus, the fact he used you as cover." Eric slapped his flat palm on the table.

"All this time he let me believe I killed a woman?" Dane asked, but the question was rhetorical.

"The Marshall probably convinced Dad it was for the best. They probably believed you'd block it out or forget all about it," Eric said. "Which doesn't mean I'll ever forgive either one of them. It just might be that they didn't know you would blame yourself."

"I don't know if anyone has ever told you this," Catalina began, "but it wasn't your fault."

"Yes, it is. I deceived my own mother. And up until a few minutes ago, believed that I killed someone and allowed it to be covered up," he defended, not ready to let himself off the hook.

"You were a child," she insisted with a calm confidence he wanted to lean into. Could he?

"I was nine," he said. "I knew right from wrong."

"You wanted your father to love you. I'm guessing you would have done anything he said to win his approval," she said. Her words made perfect sense and if it was anyone but him, he would probably agree. "Your father and grandfather used you to cover up their bad behavior. That's not your fault, Dane. You weren't old enough to go against them. They should have been protecting you, not using you to protect themselves."

"She's right," Eric chimed in. "And if anyone of us had known what was going on, we would have wrung the bas—"

Eric's gaze bounced from Dane to Catalina and back.

"Suffice it to say what he did to you was wrong on every level. The Marshall is just as to blame. But, *you* didn't do anything that any one of us wouldn't have done," Eric stated. He ground his back teeth and it was easy to see this affected him.

"All I can think is that I've let Mom down all these years by not telling her," he admitted.

Catalina's hand in his tethered him to the reality he wanted to be part of and not the one he was still trying to put in the rearview.

"This explains a lot, Dane." Eric clenched his back teeth. "I'm sorry you had to go through it alone and I'm not surprised you wanted to get as far away from here as possible the minute you turned of age."

"I turned my back on you too," Dane countered. He shook his head. "I'd do things a whole lot differently now."

Talking about the past to two people he cared about most was taking some of its hold over him away. The big secret was out and would filter through the family at some point in the coming days. He couldn't begin to process the fact Mrs. Maples was alive after believing he'd killed her all these years, stuffing it down so deep he never allowed himself to think about her. She'd survived. A weight the size of a boulder lifted off his chest.

"Thank you for trusting us," Catalina said with a voice like honey.

He nodded. He'd said enough about the subject for one day and was ready to begin to put the pieces behind him.

"I have to tell Mom," he said.

"If she walks out on Dad forever, it still wouldn't be your fault, Dane. You know that, right?" Eric said.

"Intellectually? Yes. But being the one to deliver the blow sure makes me feel responsible," he admitted.

"The only thing I want to do when I see the man is punch him," Eric said, his tone giving away just how dead serious he was.

"I think he's suffering enough right now," Dane said. He issued a sharp sigh. "To be honest, I just want to get it out in the open and then put it all behind me. I've been living my life too long bound by that secret. The chains are off. I'm ready to let it go and look toward my future." A future he hoped Catalina and her son would be part of. The only question was how?

16

An hour passed with no news on Dane's father. Catalina fixed the last bug in her program and all that was left to do was finalize the code. She looked over at Dane, who was nursing a cup of coffee. He looked different, lighter somehow.

"I've been thinking," she said.

He lifted his gaze up to meet hers and warmth spread through her.

"If Kal is trying to save his wife's family business and I sell this app to Hanson, won't Kal still search for something illegal? He won't be out of trouble, so what's to stop him from trying something else? Something we don't know about?" she asked.

"The only true way to stop him is to involve the law, which you said you wouldn't do because there's no proof," Dane said after a thoughtful pause.

"Maybe I changed my mind," she stated.

"What about the money? You need to sell the app for your and Luke's future," he pointed out.

"I know. It gets me out of this whole mess. But, what

about Kal?" she asked. "He's still in knee-deep. He still needs a magic answer and he's clearly willing to break the law to accomplish his task."

"You can turn state's witness. The government will relocate you both and investigate Kal," he said.

"I'm a witness, but I don't have proof." The fact Dane was willing to suggest such a thing caused her chest to deflate. Her going into a relocation program meant the two of them being apart. Call her blinded by her feelings for him, but she'd been naïve enough to believe something special was going on between them. It stung to find out she'd been wrong. The attraction had been real and two-sided, she was certain. What did it mean and what would come of it? Those were questions she lacked answers to. The answers threatened to shatter her heart into a thousand flecks of dust.

"My understanding is that a crime would have to occur first. I just 'suspect' a crime will occur and it's my word against his at this point without evidence," she stated as evenly as she could, considering her heart thundered inside her chest. It was good to know where she stood with Dane, though. Because she was beginning to think about what would come next between them. Apparently, no matter how much chemistry they had simmering between them, he wasn't interested in anything more.

The kisses they'd shared came to mind. She did her best to shove those thoughts aside, marking them as counterproductive in her mind.

Besides, Dane had just learned he wasn't a murderer like he'd believed for decades. No matter how upset she was about their non-future, her heart went out to him for his tragic past—a past that had clearly put him on a solitary path in life.

She stood up, needing to stretch her arms and legs.

"Coffee mugs?" she asked Eric as she passed by Dane.

"If you alert the feds, they can begin an investigation on him. There's no need to put yourself and Luke at risk," Dane offered.

She'd considered the possibility. Investigations took time. Time she didn't have.

Eric moved to the cabinet next to the sink and retrieved a mug for her. He held it out and as she took it, he leaned in. His gaze was on Dane the entire time and didn't falter, when he said, "I've never seen my brother look happier around someone. He's rough around the edges but I can see how much he cares about you."

"Thank you for saying that," she said, "but there's nothing I can do if he wants me to leave."

"Just be as patient as you can with him," he said. "I have a feeling someone like you won't come around for him but once in a lifetime, and it's my personal belief he knows it too. He's working through some heavy baggage and I'd just hate to see him lose you over his own stubbornness."

She smiled. It was easy to see how deep Eric's feelings ran for his brother. The sentiment warmed her heart even though she knew there was nothing she could do to make Dane open his heart to her. There was passion simmering between them that enthralled her as much as it frightened her. Not because she was scared of Dane in any way, shape, or form. She'd never experienced an attraction like this one in her life. Dane could hurt her in ways she knew, on instinct, would be far worse than anything she'd experienced because she could really love this man, *really* love him. Not the way she loved Lucas because that had started out as best friends, grew into something more, and morphed into more of a caregiver role as he declined.

This would be different, equals. Not her caring for Dane but in a real relationship with spark and fire, and depth like she'd never known. *If* he could go there too.

Catalina filled her mug and returned to the table, reclaiming her seat. When Dane looked at her, he arched a brow, like something about her had changed and he was trying to figure out what it was.

"Everything okay?" he asked before backtracking and saying, "I realize nothing is 'okay' right now, but are you okay?"

She could hold in what she wanted to say and pretend her feelings hadn't just been stomped on. Or, she could tell him. She'd gotten so used to holding in her feelings, always putting Lucas's first. And look where that had gotten her.

On a sigh, she said, "You told me to go into Witness Protection like it was no big deal to you. Like *I* am no big deal to you."

"You are a very big deal to me, Catalina." He reached for her hand. "I just don't know what that means yet."

On the one hand, he'd tried to offer reassurance. On the other, he hadn't given her anything to hold onto.

"I just think I deserve more than that from you, Dane." There. She'd said it. He could do with it what he pleased. Either way, a sense of relief washed over her at saying the words out loud. With Lucas, she'd been walking on eggshells the last few years, afraid to say anything that might trigger him into a depression or fit of anger. There was no way she could express any disappointment in him or suggest he was letting her down in any way. Looking back, she should have spoken up. She should have said her piece. She deserved to be heard.

On the flip side, she just couldn't push him toward a

mental breaking point and then send him back overseas like nothing had happened.

When she risked a glance at Dane, he looked at her with the most intense and pure blue eyes. And then he said, "I know you do and I'm working on it. If you can just hold on for me."

His admission caused her pulse to race and her heart to hammer. Could she wait for him to decide or had she waited enough for one lifetime? Emotion knotted in her throat making it impossible to respond.

And then her cell buzzed. Panic robbed her voice. She fumbled to pick up the phone only two people had the number to. She looked at the screen as a sense of dread settled around her shoulders like a heavy blanket.

"It's my grandmother," she said before answering the call. "Hello?"

"I'm fine, Lina. Don't listen—"

A shuffling noise came on the line. Gran's voice replaced by an unfamiliar one.

"Bring the app to your grandmother's house and leave it here. She'll be returned once we have what you're working on," a strange male voice said.

"It's not finished," she countered as her heart pounded her ribs from the inside out and fear threatened to suck her under. "It won't do any good. Tell Kal it'll be useless half-finished."

"Bring it or Granny dies. It's that simple," the unwavering voice said.

"Don't you dare hurt her," Catalina warned but the line went dead. It was bad enough Kal found her gran. It was only a matter of time before his men found Luke.

"TELL me exactly what just went down," Dane said to Catalina. Her face had gone sheet white and her chin quivered. The strength she normally displayed crumbled right before his eyes.

"He has my grandmother," she said, eyes welling with tears.

"We won't let him get away with this." Dane needed to think. "What did he ask for?"

"The app. He wants me to bring it to Gran's house, leave it, and then trust him to return her safely," she said.

Eric was already shaking his head.

"We can set a trap," Dane said. "But I don't want you anywhere near your grandmother's house."

"I have to, Dane," she said. "If they found her, they'll find Luke."

"Not if we get to him first," Dane said.

"You have your father to consider. I can't take you away from your family at a time like this," Catalina said. "Your mother needs you and so do your brothers."

"My family will understand," he countered. "We have enough folks here to cover any emergency."

"I'll go with you two," Eric stated. "There are only so many who can be at the hospital anyway. We'll get word if Dad's condition changes. There's nothing we can do by sticking around here."

"I have to notify Adam first." Dane didn't like the idea of putting Eric at risk any more than he enjoyed the idea of Catalina going with them. One look at her said there was no way she was staying behind, so he needed to figure out a plan that included both of them and minimized risk. He did his best thinking under pressure. This time was no different.

"We go to your grandmother's house and we're walking straight into Kal Sutton's hands," Dane stated, figuring that was the worst place they should be seen. There was, however, an alternative. "Which is why I have a radical plan."

"Which is?" Eric asked, rubbing his hands together. "Because you already know I'm up for a good fight."

"An eye for an eye," Dane said.

Catalina gasped. "Are you saying what I think you are?"

She was a quick study.

"We take what is most precious to Kal." Dane nodded.

"That would be his family," Catalina said. "And I'd bet my life they won't be home."

"Vancouver?" Dane asked.

"Lake house," she clarified. "And I know exactly where it is."

As much as he wanted to keep Catalina tucked away safely at the ranch, one look at her set chin and determined gaze said there was no way that was going to happen. She would strike out on her own if he didn't include her and he couldn't allow that to happen. She'd be ten times more vulnerable if he couldn't keep an eye on her. Plus, the thought of being away from her, even for a few hours, didn't do good things to his blood pressure.

How was he supposed to walk away when this was over?

THE NINE-HOUR DRIVE went by in a flash while Dane explained his plan to Catalina and Eric. The idea depended on nightfall, which they had, and a whole lot of luck. Catalina's knowledge of the location of Kal Sutton's lake house gave them the advantage they needed to go on offense. She said the place wasn't common knowledge and was less than two hours from the family home. Dane would bet money the man tucked his family there to keep them out of sight until this whole situation blew over. Sutton, however, would be home.

Dane didn't have a bone to pick with Sutton's wife and kids, but they were the best way to get Sutton. So, he would execute this mission in as kind of a manner as possible.

He pulled over to the side of the road as GPS warned their destination was coming up on the right. This region was known for its lakes and groupings of small cabins. The map in this area showed five cabins in a cluster. The Suttons would be the two-story to the far right and nearest to the trees. Of course, he had no intention of pulling onto the gravel lot so he overshot the turnoff, cut off the headlights, and parked on the shoulder.

"The best entry point is through the trees," he said to Catalina and Eric. With the three of them dressed in all dark clothing, it would be next to impossible to see them as they moved through the thicket. Dane could move without making much of a sound, thanks to his training. Eric could move through without drawing much attention thanks to a lifetime of tracking poachers on the ranch. Catalina had the least amount of training and, although she could throw a nice martial arts move if needed, her skills at being quiet in the woods weren't the same as theirs.

Dane had studied the online map of this place. He'd been able to pull up the floorplan of the lake house, memorizing every square foot. The house had been sold to the Suttons four years ago furnished. Dane committed the layout to memory.

"Are you sure one of us shouldn't stay back?" Eric asked. His brother probably figured Mrs. Sutton or one of the kids might run and he could be the safety net. Eric would also think about protecting a getaway vehicle.

"I'd rather stick together," Dane said. They didn't have decent communication tools, so he'd rather keep a visual on all three of them. "Law enforcement will be stretched thin out here. It would be bad luck to come to an officer checking out our vehicle but one of us can go a little bit ahead as a scout."

"What about a screaming kid? We have to account for noise and neighbors," Eric pointed out.

"The keys to a safe extraction are the right tools and speed of action," he reminded. "The faster we move, the better for everyone involved. Plus, there are three of us and three of them."

The weather was clear, not much to consider there. Dane had prepared as much as humanly possible in the timeframe they had to work with. He brought night vision goggles and duct tape—tape he hated to use but could be necessary.

Catalina nodded. Eric was already securing his pistol in its holster.

"All we need for leverage is one of them," Dane stated. "We get in and we get out as fast as possible."

He'd run through multiple scenarios in his mind before deciding on breaking the laundry room window and sliding inside. The door would most likely be closed and it was the furthest from the bedrooms according to the floorplan. A nondescript entry on a gravel road winded through the woods until hitting the clearing.

"Ready?" he asked, figuring they could come at the place from the lake side.

Both Catalina and Eric nodded.

The walk took eleven minutes, according to Dane's stopwatch. The lake house was blacked out, a good sign. The family SUV was tucked to the side, hidden. This cluster of lake houses wouldn't be visible from the street.

Dane reached down and touched the handle of the Ka-Bar knife strapped to his calve. Another tool he didn't want to use. As far as extractions went, this one should be easy. Those were the missions that worried him the most. Those were the ones that something or multiple things always seemed to go wrong on. Those were the ones someone died on. So, no, he didn't take anything for granted on 'easy' missions.

This was, however, straightforward. He'd done as much research as he could. He'd walked Catalina and Eric through the plan enough times to be confident they could do their part. Convincing Catalina to take one of the Sutton children in the first place had been the tricky part. He didn't like it any more than she did, but this would get Kal's attention, and they were running out of time.

Kal had Catalina's grandmother kidnapped, so the man had crossed a line that shouldn't be touched. Hardball was the only way to play by way of response. Dane had gotten a little too good at boxing up his emotions, a necessary skill for a job like his. Whereas Catalina wore hers on her sleeve. She'd protested, asked if there was any other way, and then accepted the idea hours into the drive.

There was no sign of an alarm system, but he wouldn't take anything for granted. Slowly, methodically, he checked every downstairs window in search of the telltale red dot. Found none. Then, prayed there wasn't a security camera somewhere hidden.

The window was easy to break. He did that with the butt of his Ka-Bar knife. The lock twisted and then within minutes, the trio was inside.

Rather than head to the children's bedrooms, he dovetailed toward the master, breaking with his own plan. The kids might have cell phones but at seven and nine, he doubted it and if they did, their mother most likely kept them in another room on a charger.

Stealthily, he moved beside the bed where Kal's wife slept. Her steady, even breathing the only sound in the room.

As he pulled the piece of tape from his pant leg, the floorboard creaked upstairs. One of the kids was awake. The kiddo would be in the room in few moments and traumatized for life if he or she walked into the bedroom. Dane would break his promise to make this as easy on the kids as possible. Now what?

17

Dane had to think on his feet. He shook the sleeping woman.

"Scream and you bring your children into the equation," he whispered, covering her mouth with his hand.

Charlotte Sutton bolted upright. She pulled the covers up to her neck as frightened eyes studied him. She was an attractive woman. Long raven hair, oval-shaped face, cat-like brown eyes.

"I'm not here to hurt you or your children unless you fight me on this. I need your cooperation and this can be over," he whispered through clenched teeth. "Do you understand?"

Charlotte nodded. She was trembling and he had no doubt she didn't want her children in the room.

The creak of floorboards in the stairwell caused her gasp. She tried to talk but his hand muffled the words.

"I'm going to remove my hand but if you scream, it's all over and the children get hurt. Do you understand?" he stated.

Wide-eyed, she nodded.

"Good. Tell your children to go back to bed. Now." The emphasis he put on the last word had her nodding faster.

He removed his hand.

"Ava and Benjamin, go right back upstairs. Mommy will be up in a minute," she yelled.

The pitter patter of little feet scurrying back upstairs allowed Dane to exhale. Their curiosity could very well get the best of them in a few minutes, so he needed to work fast.

"What do you want from me?" Charlotte's gaze scanned the room. Her eyes seemed to be adjusting to the darkness, and she looked like she was trying to discern whether or not this was a nightmare. Her chest heaved like she was gasping for air and her body shook.

Dane cursed. Normally, when he was in this position, he was extracting a family out of a crisis situation. They might be scared but he was the cavalry. This felt all kinds of wrong. He pictured Catalina's grandmother in his mind. The frail older woman being scared and with people who didn't care one way or the other if she lived or died.

"I need you to make a phone call," he stated with renewed determination.

"To whom?" Her confusion and the fact she was scared made him believe she had no idea what her spouse had been up to.

"Your husband," Dane said.

"We don't have money, if that's what you're after," she quickly said, like she needed to explain before Dane found out they were essentially broke.

"He has my grandmother." Catalina stepped out from behind Eric, who had been shielding her with his body.

"Catalina?" Now, there really was shock in Charlotte's voice.

"We need your help," Catalina said. "Your husband is out of control and I can prove it."

"My phone is on the nightstand." Charlotte motioned toward her left.

Catalina retrieved it and handed it to Charlotte, sitting on the edge of the bed. "He sent men to kidnap my grandmother to make me hand over an app I've been working on. He went after my family, Charlotte."

Charlotte was a quick study. She nodded as she pressed the contact on her phone.

"Someone's here and he has the children," she said into the receiver. "What have you done?"

The pain in her voice sent a shockwave through Dane.

"I don't care why you did it," she said. "You told me everything was going to be all right. You said you would fix this. Is this your idea of making it better? I have a gun to my head and your children could be killed?"

She shot a look at Dane, one he understood completely. She'd been betrayed by her husband and she, too, wanted him to pay for his transgressions. "You used my family's business, Kal. How are they supposed to pay the bills now?"

From what Dane gathered from the conversation, Kal was the one who put her family business in jeopardy, not the other way around. Interesting. Was he moving money in between companies? Getting investors and shuffling funds in a Ponzi scheme?

And now what? He decided to cut corners and sell the app under the table to get out from underneath his debt?

"Hand me the phone," Dane said.

"Know this, Kal. You brought my family into this. They won't suffer for you. I'll have no problem testifying against you in a court of law." With that, she handed the phone to Dane.

He wasn't one hundred percent certain she'd made his job easier until he put his ear to the phone.

"Don't do this to us. We're good together," Kal stated.

"Bring Catalina's grandmother to the lake house in one piece or your whole family dies," Dane said as plain as he could.

"I need time to work this out," Kal protested.

"Time's up." Dane ended the call.

"WE CAN'T ALL BE HERE when Kal arrives," Dane said.

"My children," Charlotte said. "They'll come back down if I don't go to them."

Remembering Catalina's martial arts skills, Dane sent her with Charlotte to check on the kids.

"I can stay here," Eric spoke up. "For insurance purposes. You need to go and get Catalina out of here too."

"I fully did not expect the man's wife to be in the dark about his activities," Dane stated to his brother, who immediately agreed.

Catalina returned with Kal's wife, who held her hand out. A flash drive rested on it. "This is the evidence you need. You should go before he shows up and finds a way to destroy it."

"What will I find on the flash drive?" Dane asked.

"I copied his hard drive," Charlotte said. "Actually, Catalina did. This has all his financial transactions and e-mails. I always wondered why we had to start coming out here during the week. He kept everything on this computer."

Catalina nodded, corroborating the story.

"This isn't the man I married," Charlotte said. "Kal used

to be idealistic. He was going to make money from a startup and we were going to travel around the world with our children. But something in him changed after the kids came along. I know he was involved in some high-stakes online poker. I'm guessing that's when he started moving money around to cover. It will all be on this." She held her hand up a little higher. "My father is old. He'll be sick when he learns what happened to the business he built from scratch, and it will be Kal's fault. He's not the man I married. I'm only sorry I let it go on this long. He promised everything was going to be fine. I had no idea the depths he would go."

Dane took the flash drive and tucked it inside a pocket in the lining of his waistband.

"I'll make sure your grandmother is safe," Charlotte reassured Catalina. "I promise."

"I'm staying back as insurance. You two need to get out of here," Eric said. "I'll bring your grandmother home."

"Thank you," Catalina said to Charlotte. "We'll help clear your father's name with this evidence."

The front door opened. Charlotte gasped. Shrugged. "Get out of here," she said. "Go."

Dane climbed out the bedroom window and Catalina quickly followed. It was way too soon for Kal to be home, which meant he had someone waiting in the wings this whole time in case something went down at the lake house.

It also meant someone would be waiting at the vehicle.

DANE NEEDED to get the evidence to the DA's office. One problem. It was the middle of the night. The DA's office would be closed. And Dane had no idea who the DA was in the first place.

Footsteps behind him caused him to freeze.

"Run and keep going until I find you." Dane located the flash drive before pressing it into Catalina's palm. She started to open her mouth to protest but there was no time for discussion. He shook his head and motioned past the treehouse. "Go. Now."

A mix of emotions darkened her features. She opened her mouth to speak before clamping it shut again. The internal debate quashed by the sounds of footsteps coming toward them at a decent clip.

"Make noise," he said, figuring he could use her to distract the jerk.

After one last look, she turned toward the lake and ran. To his right, there was a treehouse bigger than the one where him and Jacob used to play.

Dane had a plan and he hoped like anything it would work. He unsheathed his Ka-Bar knife from his ankle holster and palmed it. He glanced around, looking for anything he could use. Just before the lake stood a patch of oak trees. Their leaves were in full bloom, which would provide cover.

Footsteps neared. Dane had to make a judgment call as to whether or not he was on the jerk's path. It was a bet he couldn't afford to lose. He moved toward the oaks, figuring the guy would assume they'd kept going. His curiosity would have him checking the treehouse though. He wouldn't want to overlook such an easy hiding place.

As long as his gaze was focused on the treehouse, he would miss Dane hiding in the trees. A surprise attack would give him the advantage and he wasn't afraid to use his blade if necessary.

Dane climbed the tree and crouched low on a branch. He positioned himself so the thick trunk would block him from the jerk's view. The jerk turned out to be Kal Sutton, not a hired gun. Interesting. He'd been nearby this whole time. Or maybe he realized what was happening when no one showed to make the exchange for Catalina's grandmother.

Adrenaline kicked up a few more notches but Dane was used to controlling his reaction. Breathe. Smile. No matter what came at him, he could calm his racing pulse with those two reminders. He'd learned to look danger in the face and smile as part of his training.

Dane risked a glance. Kal's gaze locked onto the tree-house. Good.

As Kal bolted toward the small clearing, he ran close enough for Dane to make his move. Surprise gave the ultimate advantage. So did throwing someone off their game.

Dane called out like a wild animal. Kal's gaze immediately shifted, searching the tree as Dane came down on top of him. There was a split-second where Kal realized what was about to happen, and that he was powerless to stop it. His reaction time couldn't compete with gravity—and Dane was a force of nature.

The two rolled a few times before Kal came up on top. His stroke of luck wouldn't last long. Dane threw a punch that landed on Kal's jaw. Heard a crack. Kal's head snapped back.

It didn't take long for Dane to have Kal on his back with a blade to his throat.

"You're going to pay for what you've done," Dane managed to get out through clenched teeth. "You hurt someone I care about and you're about to learn what happens when you cross that line."

"Dane, it's okay. My grandmother is safe. She's at the lake house." Catalina's voice brought him back from a dark place—a place where he'd almost just taken a life for revenge.

But Kal didn't deserve to die. He needed to spend the rest of his life behind bars.

"He's not worth it," Catalina repeated a few times as the sounds of sirens split the air.

It didn't take long for deputies to flood the place and it took even less time for Kal and his hired hand to be hand-cuffed in the back of law enforcement vehicles.

Catalina handed over the evidence.

"Go see her," Dane said. "I'll finish up here."

It took another fifteen minutes—minutes that felt like hours—to give his statement before he joined Catalina inside the lake house. Grandmother was shaken up but going to be fine. He and Eric bear-hugged before Dane hauled Catalina against his chest.

"I can't lose you," he whispered to her. And he hoped she felt the same way.

"If someone had told me I'd fall in love with a person at first sight before I met you, I would have laughed in their face," Dane said. "Here's the thing. I know you from some-where deep inside. A place that sees more than anyone can ever realize. And I could say that I knew you from what I'd heard but that's not exactly right. It's like two souls who already knew each other and had been waiting for the day they'd be together again. That's what you are to me." He brushed the backs of his fingers against the creamy skin of her face. He could stare into her eyes forever. But right now, the urge to kiss her was an overwhelming force. He closed his eyes, dipped his head, and pressed a kiss to those tender lips of hers. When he pulled back he said, "I love you, Catalina."

Dane held his breath waiting for a response.

"You are my person, Dane." When she looked up at him, her eyes were filled with love. "You have my heart."

"I want to be with you, Catalina. It might take time for me to be the person I see in your eyes. There's still a whole lot of darkness inside me." He wanted to give her an out because the road ahead might not be as easy as she deserved.

"Then, I'll sit beside you in the darkness." Those words, spoken with compassion, broke through more of his walls.

"I can't promise it will be easy," he said.

"Doesn't matter. It'll be worth it." There was no hesitation in her voice.

Dane's heart filled with hope. Hope that he could beat these demons trying to eat him up from the inside out. Hope that he could let Catalina in, *really* in. Hope that he could have a future with her and her son. One word came to mind, *family*.

"If we're going to do this for the long haul, I'd like to do it the right way." He dropped down on one knee and took her hand in his. "Catalina Ivey, I can't believe how lucky I am to have found you. It must be fate, something I didn't believe in a few days ago. Now, I'm convinced it's real. Because I'm fated to love you for the rest of my life. I was lost before I bumped into you. I didn't realize how far off compass I'd gotten until I saw me through your eyes—eyes filled with compassion and understanding I'm not sure I'll ever deserve. And I want to make a vow before God and everybody to stand by your side for as long as I live. Will you do me the incredible honor of marrying me?"

Catalina was already nodding her head before he

finished. Her eyes were filled with tears that he hoped were from joy. "I'd be honored to marry you, Dane Firebrand."

Dane stood and kissed his future bride. The kiss, slow and tender at first, gave way to the heat that had been crackling between them since their first encounter. After Dane had thoroughly kissed Catalina until she was breathless, he said, "You make me happier than I've ever been. There's no one who compares to you and ever will. I know I can break down the rest of my walls because, in the end, I get more of you."

"There's nothing you have to do or change to be with me, Dane. You're perfect just the way you are," she said, feathering a kiss on his lips. "Aren't we all just a little bit broken?"

"Not when I'm with you," he said.

"We fit," she agreed. "You fit the broken parts of me. Together with Luke, I'm ready to start a life together."

"What if I'm not the father he needs me to be?" Dane's gut clenched thinking about the role models he had.

"I would trade my life for my son's. So, I don't mean this lightly when I say that I have absolute trust in you as a parent," she said.

"How can you be so sure?" he asked.

"Because you care too much to be anything but the father he needs. You're willing to take him in your life and love him as your own. That's true character," she said. "If he grows up to be half the man you are, he'll do just fine."

Dane thought about her words. She was dead on. Because of his experiences with the Marshall and with his own father, he knew exactly the kind of parent he wanted to be.

"People learn by example and they learn by contrast," she pointed out. "You're a quick study."

She looked at him with such trust, he believed it too. It was true that his father had been, and still was, a lousy parent. It was also true that Dane knew how hurtful his father's actions were.

Dane had gone overseas to fight an enemy he didn't know in an attempt to come to terms with the one he did. He was tired of fighting. He clasped Catalina's hand in his. "Let's go pick up our son."

"I love you, Dane Firebrand," she said. "And Luke will too."

"I really hope so because that kid is already in my heart. And I can't wait to meet my new son." He feathered a kiss on her lips. His Catalina. His family. His home.

*A*nother one bites the dust. Eric Firebrand stared at his tuxedo-wearing brother. Dane was the last person on earth Eric expected to see at the altar. Yet, there he was, dressed and ready to do just that in a backyard ceremony two days after a lake side proposal. Not only was his brother gaining a beautiful bride but her son was about the cutest thing.

No amount of cuteness could make Eric wish for the same. Becoming a family was nowhere near his agenda no matter how right it looked on a few of his brothers.

"Did you see the message on the group chat?" Dane asked.

"Should the groom be looking at his phone today?" Eric asked as his brother came over and stood beside him.

"Dad turned a corner for the good," Dane said with a playful elbow jab to Eric's ribs. "He'll need to be put on meds before he can be released from the hospital. They're planning to keep him for observation anyway. But, it's looking like he'll recover with a few days of rest and IV fluids.

"Wish I was happier about the news. Suffice it to say that I'm relieved, especially for Mom," Eric admitted.

"I'm taking this whole forgiveness thing one step at a time," Dane said.

"Yeah? How's that going for you?" Eric teased, trying to lighten the mood. No one needed to be thinking about hospitals on their wedding day.

"Let's just say that I'm a work in progress," Dane shot back. It was good to have his brother home.

"Same." Eric gave a playful elbow jab, returning the favor from a few minutes ago.

Out of the corner of his eyes, he saw something else he never believed possible.

"Well, look there," he said, motioning toward Uncle Keif, Aunt Jackie, and a handful of their cousins.

"What are they doing here?" Dane folded his arms across his chest.

"From the looks of it, bringing presents," Eric shot back, bewildered, watching as they set their offerings down on the table.

They left just as quickly and quietly.

"A peace offering?" Dane asked.

"Looks like it," Eric confirmed, still in shock.

"I'm thinking Mom might have given them a heads-up about our father," Dane reasoned.

"Yeah. It's possible. Sounds like something she would do," Eric agreed.

"Could be a Trojan horse," Dane said with a chuckle.

"Maybe this family has a chance at making peace at some point after all." Eric was in a celebratory mood, so he was going easy on them.

"Funny. I didn't realize you believed in fairy tales."

Dane's elbow scored a direct hit. Another chuckle came a second later.

Music started playing. A beautiful bride stepped onto the grass wearing a white sundress and flowers in her hair.

"This is my cue," Dane said before walking toward his future.

The wedding was simple. The vows nearly brought a tear to Eric's eye. Or maybe it was the sight of Dane with a ridiculous smile on his face as he took Catalina's hands in his before kissing the bride.

Good for Dane, Eric thought as he saw a new light in his brother. A genuine one that seemed like the real deal. It was strange to think how much could change in one summer at the ranch. With their father in the hospital, more changes were on the way. Make no mistake about it.

Life could be like that. One minute Eric was driving down the same road he'd driven down for most of his life and in the next a storm blew through, causing the entire landscape to change.

He'd never felt an emptiness inside him before like the ache in his chest right now. This, too, would blow over.

Eric and Romy's story continues here.

ALSO BY BARB HAN

Texas Firebrand

Rancher to the Rescue

Disarming the Rancher

Rancher under Fire

Rancher on the Line

Undercover with the Rancher

Rancher in Danger

Don't Mess With Texas Cowboys

Texas Cowboy's Protection (*FREE*)

Texas Cowboy Justice

Texas Cowboy's Honor

Texas Cowboy Daddy

Texas Cowboy's Baby

Texas Cowboy's Bride

Texas Cowboy's Family

Cowboys of Cattle Cove

Cowboy Reckoning (*FREE*)

Cowboy Cover-up

Cowboy Retribution

Cowboy Judgment

Cowboy Conspiracy

Cowboy Rescue

Cowboy Target

Cowboy Redemption

Cowboy Intrigue

Cowboy Ransom

Crisis: Cattle Barge

Sudden Setup

Endangered Heiress

Texas Grit

Kidnapped at Christmas

Murder and Mistletoe

Bulletproof Christmas

For more of Barb's books, visit www.BarbHan.com.

ABOUT THE AUTHOR

Barb Han is a USA TODAY and Publisher's Weekly Best-selling Author. Reviewers have called her books "heartfelt" and "exciting."

Barb lives in Texas—her true north—with her adventurous family, a poodle mix and a spunky rescue who is often referred to as a hot mess. She is the proud owner of too many books (if there is such a thing). When not writing, she can be found exploring Manhattan, on a mountain either hiking or skiing depending on the season, or swimming in her own backyard.

Sign up for Barb's newsletter at www.BarbHan.com.

Printed in Great Britain
by Amazon